E.L. ADAMS

SOUTHWEST HEAT

SOUTHWEST
SUPERNATURAL

SOCIETY
BOOK ONE

MYSTIC OWL

AN IMPRINT OF CITY OWL PRESS

SOUTHWEST HEAT

E.L. ADAMS

MYSTIC OWL

SOUTHWEST HEAT
Southwest Supernatural Society, Book 1

MYSTIC OWL
A City Owl Press Imprint
www.cityowlpress.com

Cover Design by MiblArt. All stock photos licensed appropriately.

Edited by Theresa Cole.

For information on subsidiary rights, please contact the publisher at info@cityowlpress.com.

Print Edition ISBN: 978-1-64898-268-2

Digital Edition ISBN: 978-1-64898-269-9

Printed in the United States of America

To those with a dream that always seems out of reach.

1

"I DIDN'T DO IT—I SWEAR. YOU NEED TO BELIEVE ME." BILLY 'Mick' Powers smacked his head on the table, letting out a pathetic cry that didn't crack the tough façade of Addyson Owings. Mick covered his face in his hands and mumbled his innocence repeatedly, the smell of his sweat clogging the room with body odor and garlic.

"Enough of the act, Mick," Addyson lowered her face until she leveled her gaze with the suspect. Her voice remained even, straight to the point, and held a hint of amusement. Mick's body shook, and he tightened his arms against his chest in a lame attempt of protection. "You did do it, and I'm going to tell you how."

Mick's face blanched just enough for her to feel the thrill of a win. It coursed through her veins like it always did, lighting her on fire. People told her that her hazel eyes glowed when she used her talents, but she'd never tested the theory. But when Mick's gaze widened even more and he clutched the edge of the table in panic, she began.

"You wanted a hit, that was all. Your stash lowered, and that pissed off your boss. A quick hit would help the stress. Hey, it happens, right?" she said, moving from her spot directly across the table from him to lean against the further wall. She feigned understanding, carefully masking her face to look like sympathy. "You went to Jordy's house, but he wasn't home."

Mick blinked too fast for anyone to believe he wasn't worried. He swallowed hard, the sound almost causing Addyson to cringe. But she knew better than that. She didn't give anything away. With a quick frown and tsk of her tongue, she continued with the story. "Jordy's daughter was there. Cynthia Billingsworth. She told you nothing remained in the house, correct? She tried shutting the door in your face, but you were stronger. Tell me, what did you do then, Mick?"

"I left. I told you, I left and bought food at the gas station."

"We checked cameras at all the area gas stations, and there was no sight of you at the time you indicated. Try again. What did you do?"

"It ain't my fault the cameras didn't see me. I'm sure I can find a receipt or something to prove I went there. Listen, I didn't kill Cyn. I wouldn't!" he shouted and slammed his hand on the table. Something seemed to spark to life inside him. His eyes grew mean, more determined, and he sat straighter. He gave the detective a smug grin, one that stretched across his weathered and pot-marked face, and said, "Unless you have proof, I ain't talking. I'm lawyering up."

"Fair enough." She grabbed the folder from the table and snapped it shut. He wanted to play a game, so she'd let him. She curved her lips into that smile, the one that transformed her hard features into something more feminine, softer. She knew the affect it had on men, and she only used it right before she went in for the win. It had helped her solve countless cases, and this one was no different. "I'll leave you to think about the way her glassy eyes stared at you after you choked her, how your name left her lips in desperation when you shook her hard enough to break her trachea. She loved you, Mick, and you killed her. And for what?

For some blow? Word will get out to her father, and you know what that means. But you lawyered up, so we can't work out a deal."

She didn't wait for a response before spinning around and reaching for the door. Her heart raced from the thrill of a win because she knew, in a few seconds, she'd get what she wanted—a confession. Her skin prickled with adrenaline, and she waited. *Three, two, one.* She'd barely touched the cold metal handle before he said, "How do you... Who told... Wait, don't go!"

This time, she smiled for real. *Score.*

She turned back to face him, letting him see her winning smile. "Is that the start of a confession I hear?"

"I'll talk. I'll do it. You gotta protect me, though. It was an accident!"

Addyson propped her feet up onto her desk and enjoyed a steaming cup of coffee after getting Mick to confess everything. He gave her the missing piece of the puzzle they'd needed, and she heard the familiar thud of footsteps coming to her office. A combination of smugness and confidence filled the air around her, but it never crossed the line of egotistical. She knew she was the best in the Southwest Supernatural Society Phoenix office. She'd earned her right to be here and her title. She worked her ass off, sacrificing a hint of a personal life for it, but she rarely let herself think about that. Even though she didn't have to prove herself over and over, it didn't hurt to have her boss congratulate her again. With a quick glance at the mirror she kept in her bottom drawer, she wiped under her eyes and made sure to contain her crazy auburn hair with a ponytail. Appearances mattered, and as a woman, even more so. The door creaked opened, but two men stood there. Not just her boss. She could only see strong black shoes and pants. She frowned as her brows knitted together. *Well, that's new.* She always could read a vibe, and this mysterious stranger gave nothing away. An excited, nervous energy flowed from her head to her fingertips as she sat up straighter.

"Addy, you did it again." Patricio Flores looked at her with pride and warmth—something she never experienced growing up—and her chest tightened just a little. He had been her boss for two years and demonstrated time and again that sometimes, family was who you chose to surround yourself with. "Great job, kid."

"Thanks," she replied, removing her feet from the desk to the floor. Her small office allowed her to fit everything she needed: a small closet to hang extra clothes, her desk, two chairs for visitors, and her favorite old computer chair she'd owned since college. Cracks lined the material, and duct tape covered some parts, but it fit to her curves and felt like home. A lone poster of Mission Beach rested on the wall from a trip she'd taken on her own, but that was the only artwork. She preferred plain walls most of the time as they were without distraction. Besides, artwork led to people asking her personal questions, and she didn't care for small talk. Patricio entered her office and plopped down onto one of the matching chairs across from her, giving her the perfect view of the second man. Her breath caught in her throat, words escaping her.

Cooper Braxton stood at the doorway, leaning against the wall with a casual expression on his face. His chiseled jawline and dark eyebrows sent a flicker of heat over her skin. A blast of familiarity and hurt coursed through her; she'd spent two years staring at his face, wondering why she couldn't *read* him. Two years of her life dedicated to him with the hope of something more. Two years, wasted, when he'd left her. *Crushed* her, more like. For the girl who always wanted a family, to have someone love her, he'd become the person she's trusted the most. But he left, and that part of her life ended. Well, so she'd thought. Seeing him in the flesh caused her stomach to plummet as her anxieties rose at a rate she didn't have a handle on. She surmised everyone in the room could hear her heart speed up, but Patricio sighed, drawing all their attention to him.

Remain calm. Don't acknowledge him. It took all her effort, but she dragged her gaze away from her ex and toward her boss. Patricio was safe, Cooper was *not*.

"Addy, this is Cooper Braxton. He works in Southern California. He's the equivalent of you from further out west."

Her competitive streak gripped ahold of her filter, and she arched a brow to Cooper's shoulder. She wasn't quite ready to meet his gaze yet.

"We'll see about that," she responded and did her best to look professional. She stood, reached out her hand, and waited for her ex to follow her lead. She did *not* want Patricio to know about their prior relationship. She'd worked too hard for too long to let some guy who'd broken her heart derail her career path. She glanced at his face for just a second. "Nice to meet you, Cooper."

He ran his teeth over his bottom lip, grinning ear to ear as he brought his massive hand to hers. His eyes had no business sparkling like that. "Likewise, Addy."

Did her imagination play a trick on her, or had he said her name like a dirty secret? Why did he have to wear the same subtle cologne that tickled her nose and brought back a million memories? Them kissing, them making love while they camped, them planning a life together—just for him to abandon her. She pressed her lips together in a tight line, shoving down the emotions threatening to overrule her.

She cleared her throat, ran a hand over her ponytail, and faced her boss. "Now that the introductions are over, what's he doing here?" she asked her boss, earning a chuckle from Cooper. That sound flooded her with even more painful memories. He laughed with his whole body and, for one second, hearing it reminded her of how happy she used to be back then. She'd looked forward to so much with him—a family, a partner, *love*. Now she obsessed over her career and besides that...not much else. Along with the nostalgia, anger rooted her to the floor. He *left* her, so why the *fuck* did he stand in her office smirking?

She'd worked a couple cases with Patricio in years past, and he functioned the same as she did. *Work hard, don't waste time on small talk.* She cocked a hip out and remained standing. They were in her office after she'd broken a huge case, and this was her way of whipping her dick out. Maybe a part of her wanted to rub how well she'd done for herself in Cooper's face. Better than great. *Yeah, look at me and weep, asshole.*

Patricio pulled a thick manila folder from under his arm. Her curiosity got the best of her. Was it a new case? Something bigger than the drug lead she'd just gotten? Dragging in someone from another location meant one thing—a big fucking deal. "Two families have gone missing between Phoenix and San Diego in the past two weeks. Each story is the same: They were all from here, heading to California on holiday. They checked in with family members during the drive, but none of them made it to their destinations. The local police want to bring in consultants. That means us."

"Are they connected in any way, the families?" she asked, all thoughts of her past with Cooper disappearing at Patricio's words. A new case excited her and caused her blood to pump in a different way. She was anxious to help get answers, to find the truth for concerned family members. She wanted to be the person she'd never experienced growing up—someone to fill in the gaps. The main reason she'd become an investigator was to help others, and this case *needed* her. On top of that, she loved the challenge, the excitement, the newness of a crime to figure out.

"No. The first family to disappear, the Fitzgeralds, showed up a mile past the Arizona state line. No wounds, no evidence of what happened, both parents and two teenagers were dead."

Addy pinched the bridge of her nose and let the normal wave of grief come and go, as it always did. She focused her energy on the details. "How long were they missing before they were found? What is known about their disappearance?"

"From the locals, it seems like nothing." Patricio stood, his slightly overweight belly protruding from his starched, blue, button-down shirt, and he gestured to Cooper. "We want two of our finest to tag team this case, see if you can't get to the bottom of it or help point the locals in the right direction. They are worried. They haven't found a damn clue and don't want this to be a trend."

Her gaze flicked to Cooper's, his painfully gorgeous brown eyes framed with dark lashes long enough to make her envious staring right back at her. The sparkle from earlier had disappeared, and instead, an intensity she hadn't seen before radiated from him. It seemed he took this as seriously as she did. Good. She could work with that. She nodded. "When do we leave?"

"You got your ready-to-roll bag here?"

"Of course, I do." She nodded to the small suitcase leaning against the corner near her closet. If Addyson could be described in three words, they would be prepared, efficient, and determined. She'd graduated with honors in criminal justice and been recruited right out of college—it was easy to give up any hint of a normal life when she had no family, few friends, and the guy she'd thought she'd marry had left her. She rose in ranks and worked in one of the most prestigious departments where a paranormal could work at twenty-six. To ask if she was prepared was an insult. "I'm ready to go as soon as you need."

"The SUV is stocked and equipped to leave within the hour. You and Braxton will meet up with Detective Hansen near the state border around noon. I'll need a report in thirty-six hours."

"You'll have it." She refused to look at Cooper as she acknowledged her boss.

"Great." He smiled. "Nice work on Powers. Knew we hired you

for a reason," Patricio said, tapping his fist on the desk at his departure. "Cooper and you need to debrief on the case. I'm meeting with the mayor and hopefully won't be kissing too much ass, but holler if you have any questions."

"Always do." She gave her boss and mentor a tight smile, dreading the moment she and Cooper would be left alone in her small office. She loved her area in the building—it wasn't massive, but she had her desk, two chairs, her favorite lamp she'd found on a trip to Santa Fe, and a picture from college of her with her closest friend Shivani. It felt too personal to share with him after all this time. He didn't deserve to know who she was now. He'd lost that privilege.

Cooper studied the space like it held all the answers, and the thought unsettled her. Three years had passed since she'd lain her eyes on him, and the man had aged almost unfairly. His dark hair hung from his forehead in a way that made him appear like a movie star rather than a detective. The playful tilt of his lips only looked more appealing with laugh lines around his mouth. And the worst part...his eyes were wiser. When Patricio walked out, she took another long sip of the coffee and waited ten seconds before glancing at her former lover.

When their gazes met, her heart pounded painfully against her ribcage. How dare he look at her with heat after what he did? She worked her jaw left to right, trying to find the right words when he broke the silence first.

"Addy."

She closed her eyes and let the sound of her name from his lips wash over her. The sudden desire to touch him—run her tongue over a body she knew was chiseled from long hours of dedication at the gym—shocked her. She shouldn't have uncontrolled lust for him. *It's been three years.* She'd moved on. Sure, no one had come close to touching her heart and soul, but she'd been with other men. She rubbed her lips together, dug deep to find inner strength, and met his gaze head-on.

"Cooper," she said, setting the bright purple mug down and leaning forward onto her elbows. He still stood against the wall, about two feet in front of her, and grinned the same crooked smile she'd fallen in love with all those years ago. *Keep it professional. Business first. Talk about the job.* "Seems you've done well for yourself."

"Right back at ya, babe." He sauntered to her desk, propping himself up on the side of it like he owned the place, and took his time eyeing her. His signature scent of coffee and soap washed over her, confusing her paper-thin hold on her emotions.

"You look great. Real nice."

She didn't respond. She raised a brow, pursed her bright red lips, and opened the folder Patricio had left them. It did no good to acknowledge the electric attraction between them. She knew better now, to confuse lust with trust or love, and she needed to ensure he understood she would *not* be going down that route again.

She felt his stare all over her body as she flipped through the pages. Her skin burned with awareness and desire, her mind unable to focus on the details. Her lingering attraction to him numbed her thoughts, stifled her emotions, and confused her. She'd built walls around her heart to prevent anyone from getting close, and the *one guy* who was the catalyst for said walls threw her off balance. She'd survived heartbreak, lived through it, and wasn't stupid enough to do it again. Work needed her attention. *Only work.*

The case file contained pictures of the latest family, the ones they'd found dead without any marks on them. She loved the initial part of an investigation, where anything became possible, and she wanted to connect the dots. Running her tongue on the corner of her mouth, she glanced up and found Cooper's gaze zeroing in on her lips. Her skin flushed. "What do you know about the Fitzgeralds?"

"Is that's how it's going to be between us? Not acknowledging our past for a second?" he asked, lowering his voice to that dangerously sexy tone that sent shivers down her spine. He chuckled and moved from one side of the desk to the other, invading her personal space like he used to, and cupped her chin with his calloused hands. "I've licked every part of your body, been inside you for hours, and you're hoping to look at me like a stranger you just met?"

God, the sex between them had defied expectations. Explosive. Hot. Feral. Always selfless, intuitive, and communicative; Cooper dominated the bedroom. They'd gone away to Cabo for a weekend and never left their hotel room. Her face warmed at the memory, and she curled her toes in her shoes. Heat and chemistry didn't equate to more than that—a nice lay. She dug her nails into her palms, willing her pull to him to settle down, and kept her face neutral.

"You might as well be a stranger, Cooper. We haven't spoken in years. I'm not the same woman you used to know," she said, hating how her voice rose just enough to give away her feelings. She channeled her inner badass and stood, shooing his hand away from her face and shoving him lightly in his chest. Her temper flared. Only he could ever ignite this type of fire beneath her skin. "If you think things will be anything but professional, then you need to request a different assignment. I don't know anything about who you are now, how you're partnering with our department, or what games you might try and play with me. But know this..." She moved closer to him, their mouths no more than six inches apart. She could smell his minty breath and subtle cologne. *God, he smells the same.*

"I am *the best* at what I do, and *nobody* is going to mess that up for me." She smacked his cheek twice and gave him her best smile. "I'll see you in the SUV."

2

FEISTY WOMEN HAD BEEN HIS WEAKNESS FOR AS LONG AS HE COULD remember. The more attitude and confidence they had, the more he wanted a taste of them. But Addy had stolen the show three years ago, and he'd carried the regret in his soul since he let her go. Even now, in the prime of her life, she radiated confidence and sex with every movement she made. Just the sight of her in her stiff, white, button-up and black slacks caused him to think about making her lose control—her auburn hair spread all over a pillow, her eyes half closed, and his name spilling from her lips as he pumped into her. Yeah, he'd never forgotten what a firecracker she was in bed...her sounds and the way she fell apart in his hands.

Women like Addyson Owings held themselves to the highest standards. The constant need to prove themselves gave them an unequivocal work ethic, so when she let go, it was a wonderfully explosive experience. She ended their meeting with nothing more than a tight smile, and he found himself a fresh cup of coffee before getting into the car with her. The clock read almost nine am, and the three-hour drive with just the two of them going over notes sounded like a dream. He loved the thrill of a chase—

not just with solving crimes, but also with her. He'd worked for every inch she'd given him when they were together, and it'd be no different now. His blood hummed with anticipation.

He smiled at the few agents still in the office and let his mind wonder briefly about the various skills the agents brought to the Phoenix office. Everyone knew to be employed by the SSS meant possessing a paranormal talent, but employees weren't supposed to disclose their skills to each other. The local cops still held some preconception against those from the SSS, especially if their talents helped cracked a case. It was a tough line to dance, having the public fear you when you weren't actively solving their problems. Humans weren't kind to paranormals unless receiving something out of it. Even after decades of living together, a prejudice lingered in the air. Regular citizens were pissed paranormals looked *normal* but held gifts they didn't have. Often times, people hid their true talents to live a normal life, one without getting yelled at, exposed, or bullied. Relationships between paranormals and regular ole humans were frowned upon, even though they worked. Some of the best couples he knew were imbalanced in that sense. But choosing to be in a relationship with a paranormal meant a harder life. Plain and simple. *That* he knew. But recently learning about Addy being a paranormal had changed everything.

That was why he'd left all those years ago. He'd discovered his exceptional skill at the ripe age of twenty-two, but how could he explain to her he had…powers? It wasn't acceptable to talk about that with humans. Too taboo, too dangerous. How did he tell her that he could project thoughts onto everyone in his presence? He couldn't, so he'd bolted. He hadn't wanted to put her in the position of having a harder life. It wouldn't have been fair to her. He'd felt it the right decision then, but not a day went by when he didn't think of her or the future he'd envisioned with her, and it wasn't a coincidence he'd ended up paired with her for this case. When he'd heard Addy also had supernatural talent, he'd used every card he could to get this assignment. He wouldn't stop until he won her back.

He might've acted like a fool before, but he never would again.

"Coop, heard you and Owings are paired, dude." Frasier Davidson, another SSS employee he'd crossed paths with over the past three years, walked to him and shook his hand. He didn't have powers but still worked alongside supernaturals. Each department hired a few regular agents in their division to ensure all species had a chance to investigate. The only word to describe Frasier was average. Average height, attitude, skill, personality. "She's the ice queen, man. One of the best, but intensely focused on work. I swear an investigation gets her off at night."

His jaw tightened at Frasier's crassness, but he hid his contempt for the comment and smiled at the middle-aged man. "How have you been? How's the kids?"

"Riley is heading off to college and..." Frasier kept talking, but Cooper's attention went to the slender body dressed in all black that had just left Addy's office. She'd changed clothes. *Goddamn, her body got better.* The black sweater and black jeans hugged every single one of her delicious curves that had only become more lovely in his absence. The sway of her hips called to him, and he adjusted his position on the welcome bench to hide his reaction to her. She deserved to be cherished, loved, adored, and touched, and he wanted to be that person for as long as he kept breathing. She moved with purpose, and he knew each and every muscle in her body had taken time and effort. She'd trained herself to be a weapon, and there was something hot about it. Kissing her soft skin and toned muscles years ago would have nothing on her growth now. *Damn.* He bit the top knuckle of his fist. They might call her the ice queen here, but that thrilled him. It meant they didn't know the real her beneath the badass.

Good. Less competition.

Frasier gave him an expectant look and Cooper grinned, carefully projecting his thoughts of what he wanted Frasier to see. *Remember you have to finish a report before leaving.* The chatty guy blinked a couple of times. The vacant look in his eyes and the slight buzz racing through Cooper's body gave him the satisfaction of knowing it had succeeded.

His powers worked in a strange way, but he'd learned to master every aspect of them since he left Addy. When a projection succeeded, his blood hummed with a warm energy. When it failed, a spike of cold shot through him.

Frasier grinned like a drunk and said, right on cue, "Great seeing you, man. I gotta head out to finish a report before heading home to the missus, but good luck with Owings. She's nice to look at but a real—"

"Careful what you say, Davidson," Addy appeared at the end of the hall, her full lips curving into a wicked smile that sent blood straight to his dick. She swaggered down the narrow hallway to them and leaned one shoulder against the beige wall. "It'd be a real shame if your wife knew what you spent your time watching on your phone in the garage. A real shame."

Frasier's eyes bulged out of his head, and he blushed so red Cooper expected him to burst into flame. He grabbed the coat off the back of the chair and headed down the hall.

"Bye now," she replied in a saccharine voice that fooled no one. Once Davidson had vacated the area by her office, she focused those gorgeous eyes on him. They held no anger, no heat, no hint of any emotion. Without another word, she strode past him and shut the door.

This is going well. He sighed.

Cooper ran his hand over the back of his neck and checked in with his office in San Diego on his walk to the car. Drive-by shootings had increased in the area, and without any leads in weeks, the city grew restless. He read an email from his partner, Logan Lovely, and winced at his brisk words.

Followed an anonymous tip, came up short. Bringing in Tyson for the next two days but expect you back in forty-eight hours.

Two days to solve a crime that had captured the media's attention and get Addy to give him another chance. Call him an overachiever, but he hoped to succeed at both. With one last chug of his shitty coffee, he threw the Styrofoam cup into the trash and followed Patricio's directions to the parking lot where they would leave from.

Addy stood at the back of the black SUV and didn't give him a glance as she stowed her suitcase in the rear. "Still need to be in control of everything and drive?"

"Aw, you remember," he teased. She tossed him the keys, rather hard, and he laughed. "If I recall, you prefer to be in charge of directions. Figured you could read us the file while I drove."

He placed his bag in the trunk with hers, briefly remembering one of the trips they'd taken together. She'd worn the filthiest two piece and God, they'd never left the hotel room. They'd drank and eaten, then spent hours in bed. He shivered. He'd tossed them away out of fear and regretted it ever since. He hopped into the driver's side, glad to be near her again. Even if she gave him the *"piss off"* vibes she threw his way.

She sat down in the passenger seat with the folder resting on her thighs. It was hard not to stare at her long neck, dainty features, and delicious, bowed lips he knew felt like heaven. He'd have a difficult time driving with her smelling like flowers and sin sitting next to him.

"Stop. Whatever you're doing, stop." She didn't move a muscle when she addressed him, and it annoyed him how unaffected she was. Regardless of how they'd ended, their chemistry destroyed any hope of him finding another lover like her, and a selfish part of him wanted her to admit they still had the same pull toward each other. The pulse at the base of her neck had raced when she'd first seen him, and she couldn't hide her physical rection to him. Even now, in the confines of the car, he felt the air move every time she shifted positions.

"What do you mean?" he asked, waiting for her to acknowledge him. The indifference on her face disappointed him. He knew it'd be hard to win her back, but he'd never considered the notion she could refuse him. His stomach sank, the flicker of fear numbing him for a second. He had to win her back; there was no one else for him, and he knew it. He swallowed hard and started the car. They were on the highway when he glanced at her again. Still no answer from her. He exhaled, gripped the wheel harder, and hated the way his chest tightened. "Would you set the folder down and look at me for two seconds, please?"

She sucked her bottom lip into her mouth, letting out a frustrated sigh, and crossed her legs before meeting his gaze. He didn't expect to see anger there—okay, maybe a little bit—but not the raging impatience that radiated off her. "What?"

"You've been doing a damn good job avoiding my gaze. I wanted to make sure yours were still hazel."

"They are." She blinked and studied him with tight lips and narrowed eyes. "I want to make this very clear, Cooper, I don't want to work with you. Honestly, I have no idea how you're even involved with the SSS or how this came to be, but if I didn't respect Patricio so much, I'd back out."

"You're smarter than that, Ads." At the use of her nickname, her nostrils flared, and her grip on the armrest tightened—the first signs she remembered anything about their past.

She sat up straighter and sucked the inside of her cheek into her mouth. "You're a paranormal."

"As are you," he added, fighting a grin at the red blotches forming on her face. They always showed up when she was mad, embarrassed, or turned on—and he'd bet money she *wasn't* turned on. "Funny how neither of us knew that about each other."

Learning she was a paranormal had shocked the hell out of

him. He'd left to protect her, to prevent her from having a tough life by being with him. He'd thought himself the only paranormal in their relationship, and to find out she was too? That enacted his plan to get her back, but sorrow and regret clouded his thoughts. He'd missed out on *years* with her. Missed her becoming even more badass at her job, missed her birthdays, holidays.

"I didn't know what it was, officially, until they recruited me. It's not like I kept it from you." Her tone came out hurt, and it felt like a knife to the gut.

"And you think I kept it from you?"

"I try not to think about anything from that time. My life is different, more complicated than you can imagine, and I don't care if you did hide it from me," she said nonchalantly, like their relationship didn't matter to her. The red splotches on her neck gave her away. *Liar.*

"Bullshit."

She narrowed her eyes at his aggressive tone, and he cleared his throat, hoping to rid it of any evidence of his stress. "I left because I'd learned about my powers and didn't know how to handle it."

"I don't care why you left. All I know is that you did, with nothing more than a goodbye, and that's the one part I can never forget." She gritted her teeth and took a deep breath, piecing herself back together. He admired her resolve and determination to remain tough, but he remembered everything about her—her sounds, her dreams, her worries, her heart...

He'd met his match with her. She was the strongest woman he'd ever known, and letting her go was his biggest regret. Cooper contained more confidence than the average man, and while he hadn't expected a warm welcome from her, her continuous cold attitude worried him. Going down memory lane wouldn't help but talking about work would be safe. The case. That'd what he needed to do to get her to talk. "What are your thoughts on the case so far? I imagine you've already skimmed through the details."

Her shoulders relaxed, and he snuck a glance at her slim legs crossed in the front seat. "I'd like to talk to the person who found them in the van. It's odd how there are no visible marks or cause of death."

"My instinct says paranormals." He tapped his fingers on the steering wheel and stared at her for a second. She took his breath away with her sheer beauty, not only how naturally gorgeous her features fit her face. Her intelligence, her focus, and her grit captivated him. He worked his jaw left to right and continued. "There's been an increase in crimes without explanation over the past year."

She sucked in a breath and shut the folder. "I thought the same. What made you think of them?"

"Unmarked bodies and the territory."

She pushed those pouty lips into a full "oh" shape, and desire shot through his lower belly. She clicked her tongue a couple of times before saying, "Yuma is home to a large Vampire and Wolf population. Not too far from where the bodies were found."

The painful, nostalgic memory of her making the same sound in college made his heart beat a little faster.

"Correct, but what's more, there has been an ongoing war between the two over the past five years. Started with an accidental killing. Baxter Brown is the Alpha of their pack, and a new vamp killed their youngest son. Despite the fact it was a freak accident, the pack has been at odds with the Roman clan since."

She ran her fingers over her watch a couple of times before she responded. "Do we know the status of the first family of victims, the Fitzgeralds? Were they paras?"

"That's the million-dollar question, Ads." He tapped his hands on the wheel and thought about pushing a thought to her. It'd be easy to do. He could command a simple phrase. *Open up to me.* A chill went through his veins and he ground his teeth. He refused do use his powers to win his girl back, even if it would speed things up. He might've been an asshole to her once before, but he vowed never again.

"It couldn't have been wolves." She stared at the files as she continued reading about the case. "They leave evidence. Teeth marks, claws, destruction. Their oversupply of alpha-ism forces them to take pride in their killings. These bodies had nothing visible that I can see."

"Photos from the ME in there?"

"Yup." She picked up the stack and scanned through them. Cooper glanced as best he could without taking his attention off the road. She clicked her tongue as she studied each one.

Life with her had been his happiest time. Laughter and warmth filled their days, and lust and passion claimed their nights.

He was well and truly a dumbass for freaking out about his powers and bolting, especially without talking to her. Sure, a part of him had worried they were so happy because he'd accidentally pushed thoughts onto her. That perhaps she didn't love him genuinely enough to go through life with a paranormal. He shook his head and brought himself to the present, fighting the urge to run a hand over her gorgeous hair just to make sure she was real. "Anything popping out to you?"

"No." She licked her bottom lip, and his dick twitched. He needed to get it the fuck together. "I'm not convinced it's not vamps, though. They've gotten more progressive and cleverer with how they pick their victims."

"True, but from my understanding, there have been many laws and regulations introduced about using humans for blood. The general public still fears them, though. If they did this, it would set them back from the tiny progress they've made. I've talked to the Lead Roman, and Reginald wouldn't condone this."

"Reginald?" She laughed. "That is the least fearsome name I could imagine."

Her laughter felt like a hug around his soul, and he smiled. "He's terrifying in person, but you're right, the name is not ideal. I'd go with Lucius or Damien or Malachi."

"Mm, I think Vlad works."

"That's the equivalent of a white girl named Karen," he said, enjoying the way her lips curved. Making her smile was his favorite pastime, and he would do whatever it took to see it again. "Or Becky."

She snorted. "You've made your point well, Coop."

Coop.

The one syllable caused an explosion inside his chest. It appeared the walls were crumbling around her heart, and he intended to plant himself in there before she reconstructed them. "You've done really well for yourself, Ads. I'm proud of you."

Her face turned the slightest pink before she sat up straighter and removed any hint of joy. "I've worked hard."

"I have no doubt." He wanted to reach over, grab her hand or squeeze her thigh, but he wouldn't cross her boundary. He didn't want her to feel uncomfortable in any way. "You've always been the hardest working person I've known."

"Yeah, well..." she trailed off, furrowing her eyebrows. "Thanks."

"You're welcome."

It pleased him to see her soften. It was a step closer to her letting her guard down. She cracked her knuckles and narrowed her eyes at him for a second with an odd expression on her face. A tingling sensation started along his skin, like tiny fingers tickling from his feet to his head. "Ads, what are you doing?"

"Seeing something."

"Are you trying your powers on me?" he asked, unsure if she could. The bottom of his gut hollowed out, worried she'd be successful. He didn't have a clue what her powers were—paras rarely shared if they weren't in a group like wolves or vampires— and he didn't like the fact she could have leverage on him.

"Yes." She ran her finger along her chin and tilted her head to the side a little bit. "You look nervous, Cooper."

"I'm not," he said, hoping his voice didn't give away his real worry.

She hummed in response and broke out into the biggest grin he'd seen since he'd walked into her office. The full force of her smile knocked him on his ass. It took up her whole face. The straight white teeth, the joy radiating from her hazel eyes, the crow's feet showing she tended to live a life with happiness. He wanted to take a picture of her like this.

But the joy left when he deciphered what had made her so happy.

Fuck. He gritted his teeth together. "Any chance you're going to share with me what your powers are?"

"Not a chance in hell, Braxton. Not a chance in hell."

3

ADDYSON WOULD RATHER LICK THE BOTTOM OF HER SHOE THAN admit she'd lied to Cooper Braxton. Sweat broke out on his forehead, and his jaw tightened when he thought she'd used her powers on him, and she took the opportunity life handed her on a platter. She would mess with him the entire time.

Make him think she could control him, steal his thoughts, or project images into his brain. Paras had all sorts of powers that couldn't be contained or controlled, and her mind went wild with ideas.

Cooper remained uncharacteristically quiet for the rest of the drive, until they pulled into a restaurant on the Arizona/California border. They walked into the diner, and she scanned the place. The detective had to be the man sitting alone with three coffees. She approached him, Cooper right behind her, and her body hummed with acknowledgment of being correct. His nametag read *Detective Hansen*. Addyson slid into the booth first, smiling at the older gentleman. "I'd say nice to meet you, but given the circumstances, let's get right to it."

"Appreciate the lack of small talk. Hate the concept of it," he replied, drawing his gaze from Addyson to Cooper. "Braxton, hear you're a real charmer."

"I have moments." Cooper smiled and shook the man's hand. "I'm surprised you wanted to work with SSS. You're a bit of a traditionalist."

"True, but there hasn't been a damn clue as to why one family is dead and another is missing. My pride is important, but not so much I can't ask for help when it's needed. Paranormals freak me out—I don't like my mind being messed with—but my boss trusts your boss, so that's enough for me."

"Tell us what you know about the Fitzgeralds," Addyson said, pulling out a notebook and pen from her bag.

"A woman after my heart. All work." Hansen held up his coffee mug and started talking. "Dad is an engineer at a car plant, mom's a librarian for an elementary school. Oldest son attended college in Flagstaff to be a teacher, and the daughter was as nice as can be. Majoring in communications at Arizona State. They didn't have any known enemies, owed no money, were involved in zero scandals that could be found by our men. They have no criminal records and seem to be a nice family. Went to church every Sunday, kids played sports growing up, and mom and dad took yearly vacations, just the two of them."

Addyson felt the hum inside her veins as the detective spoke. He wasn't lying. The images in his head were clear and lacked any malice. "Where did they go on vacation?"

Hansen checked his notes. "Hawaii, mostly. They owned a timeshare there."

"Is the church they attended in the notes?" she asked, writing down all the places they could've come into contact with supernatural beings. "And the elementary school?"

"All in the file." He frowned, and his large, graying brows sat like caterpillars over his tired eyes. "I don't get it. In my life, crime is often about money, pride, protection, or drugs. This new world with paranormals and all sorts of new ways to kill stumps me. I always struggled with when to retire, but I'm leaning more that way every day."

Cooper pushed onto his elbows and spoke in a softer tone. "Paranormals have been around for decades—they've just stopped hiding. The world needs men like you, Hansen."

The older man blushed, and Addyson hid her smile. Cooper oozed charisma. He made people feel appreciated and did so in a way that never felt fake. The genuine praise flustered her, and she swallowed down her fondness for him. He'd left her. He'd crushed her. Attraction could linger even with a broken heart.

She'd be in trouble if she didn't remember that.

"I put all the transcripts of interviews in the file. Neighbors, co-workers, the guy who found them... Nothing stands out. Not a damn thing." Hansen rubbed the palms of his hands over his eyes. "It's pissing me off, frankly."

"What about the other family? The one that's missing," Addison asked, prodding into his mind to see what he saw. The open honesty from the Fitzgeralds was replaced with an almost dark, storm-like cloud.

"Davidsons." He grunted. "The complete opposite of the Fitzgeralds. Parents have a rap sheet of petty things. Oldest son has been arrested twice, daughter has dropped out of high school and sells drugs. All four of them have done time at some point."

Addyson frowned. "You speak to their neighbors and co-workers?"

"Sent some guys to try, but no one talks to us in their neighborhood." Hansen took a large sip of coffee and flagged down the waitress. "I know I should cut back on caffeine, but at this point in life, if coffee is what kills me, I could think of a million other ways I would rather not die."

"Fair point," Cooper said, tracing his finger over the top of his mug. "You seem to not like the Davidsons, Hansen."

He barked out a laugh. "They are lowlives, and I don't think too many people will miss them. Don't get me wrong, I want to find out where the hell they are and provide justice because that's who I am, but they don't have a lot of friends around here, that's for damn sure."

Addyson felt the hum in her veins as she searched deeper into his mind. She sensed he didn't understand or particularly like paras, but if he was wasting time by hiding something, she'd figure it out. "Were you the arresting officer on... What was the father's name?" She scanned the second file. "George. On any of George's priors?"

"Yes, but I don't see how that applies to this case."

"Not saying it does. Just getting a bigger picture." She chewed her lip, quickly reading the notes about him. "He bad-mouthed police often."

"Yes. He was a dick. Awful father, husband, citizen." Hansen sighed and suddenly looked years older than he had ten minutes ago. "He probably involved himself with something he shouldn't have. What I'm trying to figure out is how he roped the Fitzgerald's into this. I know they are innocent in this entire thing. I'd bet my pension on it."

"Who was reported missing first?"

"The daughter, Kayla. Waitress at a diner and low-level drug dealer."

Cooper tapped his knuckles on the table and nodded a couple of times. "Thanks for the coffee and information. Are the bodies still at the morgue?"

"Yes. I can escort you there when you want to go." He started to move out of his seat, but Cooper stopped him. "Tomorrow would probably be better. Lisa has her hands full right now, just came from there this morning."

"That's fine. We need to review your case notes and might interview some of the same people you did." Cooper stood to his full height, almost a foot taller than Addyson, and she ignored the heat radiating off him as she slid by him toward the door. Every part of her gravitated toward him, and she cursed her hormones. Cooper was off-limits. If she had to get it tattooed on her eyelids for the duration of the case, she would. She sucked in a breath when Cooper gently placed a hand on her lower back as she passed and hated how goosebumps exploded down her body.

Focus. She stilled and smiled at Hansen. She wanted to say something to ease his mind but remembered he hated small talk.

"We'll figure it out, Detective. You don't have to understand us, but we're the best."

"I'm counting on it."

She waited a beat before throwing a five on the table and exiting the small retro café. Fast food was her least favorite option, and the job tended toward it too much. There was a grocery store up the road that would have fresh salads, and they could use a snack run anyway. She held the folders to her side and walked toward the SUV when her veins began to hum, startling her.

This felt unfamiliar. It crept into her veins and soul, a steady thud matching her heart. Worry etched itself to the back of her neck, her instincts taking over as she scanned for whatever caused the sensation. It unnerved her.

Cooper stilled next to her, and she wondered if an internal alarmed blared for him too. He moved a step ahead of her, positioning himself in front of her body. He reached one hand behind him, resting it on her hip as he tensed. The muscles in his back rippled against his shirt, and sweat dripped down his neck. They stood there, as a team, for a few seconds before the reason showed themselves.

Vixens.

Three of them—all equally beautiful enough to cause people to stare—exited a blue truck, chilling expressions on their faces. Their roles as modern-day sirens made them dangerous. Anyone —humans and paranormals alike—attracted to women stood no chance against their beauty.

"Ladies," Cooper drawled in a sexy tone that made her blood turn to ice. "How do we do?"

The middle one blew him a kiss and laughed as she sauntered toward the pathway they stood on. "I can smell a cop when I see one. But aren't you sexy?"

"*Detective*, beautiful."

"Doesn't matter. You're all the same to us." She practically purred when she talked, and her gaze lingered on Cooper's face before landing on Addyson. She reached out and traced along her jaw. Addy kept her expression neutral, body ready to fight if needed. She didn't trust Vixens one bit.

The woman licked her lips as she said, "Gorgeous skin, honey."

"Thank you," Addy replied, confused as hell. What was the motive here? "Is there a Vixen colony around here?"

"We're traveling." She giggled like she found the question hilarious and moved her finger to Cooper's chest. She dug her nails into it, and Cooper's eyes heated. Something sick and green exploded behind her ribcage. Jealousy had no place in her head or heart—yet seeing this Vixen touch Cooper made her clench her fists. Rationally, she knew Cooper couldn't help his attraction. Their use of sexual prowess made headlines all the time. But she'd rather not witness it. Her lip curled up.

"What brought you to this small town? Judging by the folder in your hand and this handsome man's expression, it isn't a lovers' trip."

Addyson debated what tactic would be best. Did she admit the truth or try to get answers from them? The timing of their visit seemed fishy. Three Vixens in this small town? She cleared her throat and gestured to the folders.

"It is not." She met the Vixen's transfixing gaze. "In fact, do you know anything about the Davidsons?"

Addyson noticed the slight change on her face. She blinked and lost the gooey expression Vixens tended to wear. Her weight shifted left to right before she said, "I've never heard of them. Are they paras?"

Addyson felt her skin grow hot as she prodded the Vixen's thoughts. *Holy shit.* Flashes of the Vixen's recent whereabouts replayed in her own head, and it took all her control not to react. *Perfect.* She found the information she wanted and needed to find an exit. "We're not sure. Potentially. Either way, we're trying to find out what happened to them."

"I can ask around." She slid next to Cooper, and Addyson's jealousy reared its head again. She needed to break the spell she held over Cooper before she did something stupid, like punch her.

"It would be appreciated. Here, let me give you my card." She patted down her pocket even though she knew she didn't have cards with her. Forcing the victim to break eye contact was the only way to stop the spell. "Cooper? You have yours?"

He shook his head but continued to look at the Vixen. The longer he stared at her, the more he fueled her power. Addyson reached out and gripped his hand. When she intertwined her fingers with his, it felt like an electric bolt crashed down on them. Her body hummed in response to his touch, and she didn't have to pull him away. He snapped out of the trance. "Addyson," he said, worry lacing his tone.

"Ah, maybe it is a lovers' trip after all. So long, handsome." The Vixen snapped her fingers and the other two followed her into the diner. Addyson kept an eye on them through the window and watched until they sat down across from Hansen. *Interesting.* Yes, her instinct was right. The timing seemed suspicious.

She tried to remove her hand, but Cooper's grip tightened, and he pulled her to him. Her breath caught in her throat at the tender expression on his face, and she sucked in her bottom lip to prevent herself from saying anything she'd regret. It hadn't been half a day and the feelings she'd thought dormant kept rising to the surface.

He stared into her eyes, his dark ones intense and filled with guilt. "That didn't mean anything."

"I know," she said, unsure why he'd defend himself. He could look and flirt and be with whoever he pleased. She shook her head, but he placed a hand on each of her shoulders and squeezed. It warmed every part of her body despite the raging Arizona heat.

"Look at me."

She was powerless when he touched her and spoke in that low voice. "Cooper," she started, hating the need leaking through, but she had no idea what to say.

I still have feelings for you.

I never got over you.

I never will get over you.

I'll never forgive you.

She slammed her mouth shut and waited.

His eyes became clouded as he lowered his lashes against his cheek, wincing before moving his hands to cup her face. The rough tips of his fingers reminded her of all the nights they'd been together without a care in the world. She shivered from the memory.

He blew out a long breath, his lips twisting into a scowl. "My first time with a Vixen."

"Ah, Vixen cherry," she said, hating how it pleased her to see him embarrassed. The man contained confidence in spades, and seeing him vulnerable did something to her heart. "The great Cooper Braxton fell to their charms."

"It didn't mean anything. I swear." He ran his thumbs over her cheeks, and she wanted to lean into the embrace—even for a second—but wouldn't allow herself the privilege.

"I know." She moved out of his reach and jutted her chin toward the car. "Let's go. I got some information from your new lady friend."

He growled, strode to the driver's side, and hopped in. Air

conditioning blasted her face when he started the car. She sighed in relief before sharing the news. "This might be worse than we thought."

"What do you mean?"

"Lover girl is here for a reason."

"Care to tell me what that reason is, Ads, or do you enjoy riling me up for the fuck of it?"

4

THE WOMAN INFURIATED HIM IN THE BEST WAY. SHE TOOK HER TIME pursing her lips and inhaling for a few seconds, and he thought about leaning over the center console to kiss the truth out of her. They used to play that game before he'd ruined it all, and he wondered if she still enjoyed the same places being teased. He couldn't disguise the desire in his voice and decided he wanted her to know. Not acknowledging their lingering attraction would be stupid. It still burned brightly between them. "Addy, I will kiss every part of you to get the truth, and we both know how easily you'll fold."

"You lost the right to kiss me when you abandoned me, Braxton," she fired back, surely not realizing she'd laid her cards out for him to pick up. He welcomed the blip of emotion—her anger meant she cared, and her caring meant he might still have a small chance.

Abandoning her was the ultimate betrayal in her book. Her parents had left her, most of her friends had left her after she'd declared herself a paranormal—and he knew because he'd kept tabs on her the past few years—and the tough woman had had no choice but to harden up. "Just think of sharing the information as the quickest way to get rid of me."

Her entire body relaxed, the wrinkles on her forehead disappearing. It was clear she'd do whatever she could to solve the case faster, which meant getting rid of him.

She pushed some strands of hair that had wiggled loose behind her ears. "Lover girl is here to find out how much we know about the crimes. She's working for a guy named Nate. Unsure what his power is or who he reports to, but this Nate guy is driving the ship."

"And how did you get this information, Ads?" he asked, assuming she could read minds. If she could, he'd let her read his front to back. He held no secrets and wanted her to feel his regret. That he pined for her and wished he could go back in time.

She flared her nostrils for a second before raising one perfect brow. "How do you think?"

"She sat you down and told you when she entranced me? You've been best friends for years and she sent you a letter explaining everything? Come on, Ads. I want you to tell me. *Trust* me."

"You're so frustrating." She brushed her magnificent hair off her shoulder and groaned. "You damn well know how I got it. Stop being a pain in the ass."

"Fine, don't share your full ability. I trust you. But let's talk about Hansen for a second." He shifted in his seat to face her. "I have a theory."

"Let's hear it."

"Want to try kissing the truth out of me?" he said, earning an eyeroll from her. He loved her no-bullshit attitude and hoped he would break down her walls. "Just kidding, I don't want to kiss you. I haven't been staring at your lips the last hour anyway."

She sighed. "Sure."

"I don't." He didn't care if he acted like a teenage boy desperate to get a girl to like him. Addyson rendered him to a complete idiot, and he would admit it to the entire world. "Really, you're not my type."

"Okay, liar." She laughed and licked her lips—a telltale sign she was turned on. "You're saying if I leaned over the console and stroked your hair, pulling it just a bit, you wouldn't suck my lip into your mouth?"

Jesus. This backfired. His cock stiffened in his pants, and he cleared his throat, hoping with all his soul that she would take the bait. "Try and see what happens. *Please.*"

She released a pent-up breath and scooted an inch closer to him. All the air in the car seemed to disappear, and his breath came in choppy waves. The leather chair squeaked when she moved another inch, and he tensed. She brought her hand up to his face and combed her fingers through his hair, rubbing his scalp to the point he groaned. God, he'd missed her touch. His entire body shivered from the contact, and it took all his effort not to close the distance between their mouths.

"Still don't want to kiss me, Coop?" She placed a foot under her ass, giving herself even more access to him and bringing her mouth closer. Her nails dug into his skin and her breath hit his face. He couldn't focus on a damn thing except the curve of her lips, the way her eye lashes framed her hazel eyes. Something plucked deep in his chest. His throat barely worked when he swallowed, but he remained still. She put on this show, she could end it.

She leaned closer, brushing her lips across the corner of his. *Fuck.* Such a tease.

"What about now?" she asked, her voice throaty and husky. His fists remained tight at his side, and his lips, unparted. He wanted to sink into her, kiss her senseless, take his time reacquainting himself with her body. She nipped the skin right next to his cheek and laughed. "You're out of words. This is new."

"Ads," he whispered, beyond desperate to see if her lips still felt the same. He craved to taste her. Devour her. Have her. Her hair smelled the same—vanilla—and the wave of feeling settled almost knocked the wind out of him. She felt like *home.*

"Answer the question," she replied in a honey voice full of lust.

"Kiss me," he demanded, intent on not making the move. He knew if she planned to let him back into her life, she'd decide the when and how. She wore the pants, ran the game, and would be the one to cross the line. He refused to do any harm to any progress they made, but it took all his willpower to not yank her against him. But the second he'd said the words, she pulled back and laughed.

"I knew it. Reverse psychology won't work on me, Braxton." She ran her fingers over her lips as she stared out the window, but it didn't hide the massive blush running down her neck. He loved that flush of her creamy skin. Especially when he gave it to her.

He was hard as a rock, turned on to the point it pained him, but he barked out a strangled laugh. "Well played, Ads. Well fucking played."

"Tell me about Hansen."

"Give a guy a minute. You're sexy as fuck, and my dick is so hard thoughts aren't forming yet." He put both hands on the wheel and squeezed, thinking about anything in the world other than the way her breasts filled out her shirt or how her breath smelled like coffee and mints. *Nope. Not working.*

She glanced down, one of her perfect eyebrows arching up as she stared at his bulge. The woman needed to stop it with those heated looks fucking pronto. "Addy," he warned.

Her eyes lit up with glee and she wetted her bottom lip with her tongue. "Not helping the situation."

She smirked.

He ran a hand across the back of his neck and thought of disgusting things.

Death. Drugs. Donkey. Dung.

"Do you always use D words when trying to settle down?" She

stifled a giggle.

"Didn't realize I'd said words out loud." He snuck a glance at her and her smiling face from getting him all worked up. "Stop looking at me like that. It doesn't help."

"Like what?" She nibbled on the corner of her lip, drawing his attention to it, and he cussed.

"You're cute and shit." He faced forward and focused on the window where Hansen sat across from the Vixens. He shivered, hating how he'd lost all control when they'd turned the charm on. He preferred control in all things in his life, and the siren power freaked him out. He took a few deep breaths before talking. "Okay, I think the Fitzgeralds are nothing more than a distraction."

"Meaning what? Someone killed four humans for no other reason than to throw the scent off the Davidsons? How ruthless and cruel."

"Yes. You heard how much bias Hansen held when he talked about the good family versus the bad. Regardless of its merit, it was glaringly apparent."

"So whoever is behind this knew that about him. That he would focus the majority of his search on the picture-perfect family rather than the one with problems."

"Let's see. Pull up your phone and do a search of the news coverage." He withdrew a hand from his from his pocket and didn't hide the fact he was still hard in his jeans. His body heated again from her teasing. *The job. Focus, you dumb idiot.* His voice came out hoarser than before. "You ever use those powers to solve a crime?"

"My paranormal ones? All the time."

"No, that seduction act you just pulled that almost killed me."

She bit her lip and wiggled her brows. "Nope. That was a special occasion to get back at the man who broke my heart."

Ah, fuck.

Instead of responding, he took the jab to heart. Literally. He deserved it and hoped the more she released her anger, the more they could focus on the future. He'd gladly take whatever she gave him. If she wanted to fight, he'd let her win. If she wanted to yell or hit him, he'd lay down and close his eyes. He couldn't handle indifference, though, that would actually kill him.

Returning to the task at hand, he scrolled through the news stories and found the trend he'd assumed he would. "Most of the coverage is about the Fitzgeralds."

"But it's interesting that the Davidsons haven't been seen for weeks. Someone reported the daughter missing first after not showing up for a shift at work three weeks ago. The Fitzgeralds were only reported missing a week and a half ago and found quickly."

"I stand by my theory. We need to talk to the lead on the Davidsons' case."

"Thinking the Fitzgeralds were killed for the sole purpose of distraction?"

"Exactly."

"That's beyond horrible if it's true."

"Ads, you know how brutal the world can be. This isn't that shocking." His mood turned grim, and he indicated to the folder with his chin. "Who's the lead?"

"Hansen oversaw it, but the first responder was Fisher Hale."

"Want to go talk to Mr. Hale?" he asked, already starting the SUV. "Or should we get food first?" He remembered how hangry she became if she didn't eat. She preferred protein and potatoes, and it pleased him when she nodded.

"Food then Fisher."

"That's my girl," he said, so easily he forgot three years had gone by. Addyson sucked in a breath, and he shrugged. "Regardless of what happened, Ads, you always have been and will be my girl. No one has *ever* compared to you."

"Don't say that shit, Cooper."

"Why not?"

"Because it'll make it harder to push you out of my mind when we crack this case."

"I want to be in your mind, babe. I want you thinking about how good we were together so when I ask to see you again, you'll say yes." There, he'd put it on the line.

"Bold statement."

"I'm done fucking around. I've waited long enough to try and get you back, and you're stuck with me until this case is done." He hated that they only had another forty hours together before he planned to go back to his life in San Diego. What *really* waited for him there besides his partner and job? Sure, he loved what he did, but his one-bedroom apartment sat empty, lacking life and energy. His parents lived on the east coast where he saw them twice a year. He'd meet a buddy for a beer once in a while, but everything else was going through the motions. Addy held everything he wanted: a partner, someone to build a life with, somebody who understood him. "Now, do you want chicken or steak?"

"Grilled chicken salad," she replied, her voice going soft for a second. "I'm not sure I can trust you again, Cooper. It was the hardest thing in my life, getting over you."

"Well, I've *never* gotten over you. I've been existing, trying to figure out how to get things back on track. If you think I left and had a grand ole time, you're wrong. I went undercover for two weeks. I couldn't afford to think about you, but every day, you crossed my mind anyway."

He pulled out of the diner parking lot just as the Vixens exited, and he didn't miss the way they lowered their heads and focused on the car. It wasn't his intention to plan their exit at the exact time, but it didn't hurt. He wanted Nate and whoever the hell else was involved to be weary. He and Addyson were more than equipped to handle any shit that came their way. They were each the best in their own SSS office, but together they were bound to be even better.

"Fresh or from a restaurant?" he asked, remembering her

affinity for fresh produce almost all the time. They'd taken trips to the farmer's market every weekend, then spent the days naked in bed. He'd had it *so good* before he fucked it up.

"We can stop across the street."

They parked the SUV and walked into the store in silence. He watched her scan the fresh produce and pick up an already made salad. She also grabbed an extra one and a large bottle of water. "You want this one?"

The fact she offered made him smile. "Yes, please."

She rolled her eyes but couldn't hide the smirk growing on her full and perfect lips. He waited in line with her at the cash register and used his ability to have the three people in front of them believe they forgot an item. She looked at him with a curious expression. "Wow, they all exited the line. Crazy."

"What a wild coincidence." He winked, and she pursed her lips.

She leveled her gaze at him and bought the salads and water, swaying her hips as they walked outside. "We can eat in the car."

"Sounds good to me." He went to grab his keys from his pocket but felt a nervous energy cloud the air. Addyson kept walking, so he reached out to hold on to her wrist. "Wait."

She froze.

Cooper moved around her and stared at the SUV. Nothing seemed out of place. There weren't footsteps or a neon sign that said *DANGER HERE*. The thoughts of people around them startled him. "Ads, can you see if there are any witnesses right now?"

"Witnesses to what?"

"Something is off with the SUV. I feel it. I don't know what, and I'm asking you to make the connection." He kept his voice low, and his hand remained on her arm. She tried to move in front of him, but he stopped her. "Stay behind me."

"I can take care of myself, Cooper." She huffed and squinted her eyes at the surrounding vehicles. He tightened his grip on her and pulled her closer. "Coop..."

"You can take care of yourself, I know. But I can't live with myself if something happens to you. So, appease me for a few minutes until we know the threat." He pushed the hair away from her ear and felt her shudder against his touch. "You getting anything?"

"Vixens followed us and put a device under the right wheel." She sighed and relaxed into his arms and, for one second, he held her. She smelled of vanilla and he wanted to press his nose along her neck for a solid hour to refamiliarize himself with her. But he did no such thing.

"Any idea what type of device?"

"No one stood close enough to see. All the men were under their trance. Our best witness happened to be a nine-year-old." She frowned and let out a shaky breath. "We need to get the parking lot evacuated. Now."

"I'll ring Hansen." He called him within a minute, then he put in an order for a unit and started ushering pedestrians away from the SUV. "Get back into the store for the time being, okay? Everything is fine. This is routine."

He planted the thought into as many people as he could. *Wait in the store for thirty minutes. Browse the dessert aisle. Use the bathroom. Get a coffee.* He didn't have to do much more before he projected his thoughts to the people driving in. His shoulders tensed as he focused on each individual driver. *Park far away. You need extra steps. Head to a different store.* Helping people clear the area wasn't new but having Addyson around during it was. His skin felt too tight against his body every time he glanced at her. She ushered people inside, her face stoic yet friendly. His heart pounded against his ribcage as he tried not to think about something happening to her.

He knew her skills matched his, and she'd done a great job making a name for herself, yet it did nothing to ease his worry. He needed her safe. End of story.

The squad arrived as Addyson made her way toward him. Her

cheeks were flushed, her eyes focused, and damn, she couldn't have been more attractive. She jutted her thumb over her shoulder. "Another wild coincidence that people just...went into the store."

"Just as wild as you figuring out what happened," he replied, pulling her into a hug. He expected her to go stiff or yell at him. He did not expect her to go soft and embrace him back. She moved her arms around his waist and squeezed him. Maybe it was the adrenaline of the job, the flirting, or the nostalgia, but he felt like he could breathe again with her pressed up against him. "Goddamn, I missed your hugs."

"I'm still mad at you, but I've decided I don't want you hurt," she said into his chest where her face pressed against his shirt. He rested his chin on top of her head and enjoyed the moment. The way her hands dug into his back, gripping his shirt between her fingers. The sounds of traffic and sirens filled the air, but for a few seconds, he forgot all about the case and focused on her. With more officers arriving, he let go. Addy hated DPA, and doing it on the job? She'd likely stab him if he ruined an ounce of her well-earned respect. His heart ached and his chest tightened when he broke the hug.

"We did the right thing." He rubbed his hand up and down her back as the crew prepared to search their SUV. They wore hazmat suits, and one took lead, controlling the rover. Cooper never ignored his gut and, sure, if this turned out to be nothing, then they could all laugh at him. He'd prefer that. His ego could take it. But to ignore the tingling feeling that something terrible was about to happen? He refused.

The cover might discover nothing more than a GPS, but he wasn't about to risk any of them. This shit went deeper than a paranormal war, and his gut told him they were just touching the surface.

"I know." She gave him one more squeeze before releasing him and straightening her posture. She cleared her throat, ran a hand over her shirt, and shifted her head side to side. The brief moment of softness left her face, and she jutted her chin toward the leader of the bomb squad. "Let's go see what they discover."

They stood off to the side and watched the team work, speaking into radios as the rover slowly wheeled toward their SUV. Cooper's pulse raced as the arm extended under the car and, briefly, he thought about keeping his hand on Addy in the event he needed to shield her from whatever they found. Minutes went by, his muscles tensed, and his jaw clenched. Then the lead approached them. His facial expression told him the answer he'd suspected. "We found a homemade bomb."

"Jesus." He rubbed the back of his neck and met Addyson's eyes. This upped the stakes. They weren't just looking for a missing family anymore. They'd added a potential killer to their list of people to find. "Are we good to use the SUV now?"

"We just need to take statements." The man waved over a stern-looking woman wearing an expression on her face that almost made him whimper. She took lead and divided them all into pairs and placed them in different areas. The process took an hour longer than he'd anticipated. It wasn't until midafternoon that they were on the road again, salads in hand and a new truce settled over their past.

"Have you almost died before?" Addy asked after they'd been driving for ten minutes. Fisher had agreed to meet with them at his precinct, a twenty-minute drive from where they were.

"Define 'almost'."

"Been shot, been in intensive care. That sorta thing."

"I've been in situations where I thought I had seconds to live, but nothing like you've mentioned."

She frowned, picked the meat out of her salad, and ate it. "What would you rate the bomb situation? Would that rate as close?"

"I'd give it a six out of ten." He shrugged and reached over to squeeze her forearm. It felt so natural, and the fact she smiled when his hand touched her skin made him want to fucking sing. Her smile knocked him off balance when she directed it his way. Her gaze softened. "You worried, Ads?"

"I haven't hid behind a desk or anything, but I tend to work regular cases with less risk. Drug busts, manslaughter, break-ins. Missing people now and again, but they were clean-cut. No lingering threats held over my head. It's been three years since I've been in this world with unlimited possibilities, and I'm a little worried."

"Don't be. You have the brains and the power. Trust your gut. Patricio would not have given you this case if he didn't believe in you." He chose not to mention the fact he didn't think Patricio knew how bad this could be. "We're a team now."

"Yeah. I guess we are." She gave him a small grin and continued to eat the protein minus the rest of the salad. He snorted, and she gave him a sly look. "Leaves don't sound appetizing right now, okay? Don't judge me."

"I would never."

"You are. Admit it."

"Nope." He chuckled. His face hurt at the realization of how much he'd laughed with her. Joy rarely came the last three years, and after just half a day with Addy, his life improved. "I would never make fun of you for ordering a large ass salad and then picking the protein out of it. Never."

"Jerk," she mumbled but kept lifting out the pieces she wanted. "What's your take on all this?"

"That I'll save you in a dramatically cool way, and you'll realize you still love me and give me another chance."

"The case, Cooper. What is your take on *the case*?" Humor laced her tone, and he considered that another win.

"Testy. My plan must be working." He winked again and smiled wider when she covered up a snort by pretending to cough. "Well, we need to find out what Fisher knows. That will lead us to why this Nate guy sent Vixens to blow us up."

"Vixens aren't known to be violent or engage in any turf wars. Every one I've met or known is pleasant, almost always with a 70s vibe of peace, love, sex. Even when you were drooling, I didn't pick up any negative intent."

"But your *witness* saw them plant the device."

"Yes." She bared her teeth in a smile at his strong use of the word witness. "We need to figure out why."

"Along with what happened to the Davidsons and why the Fitzgeralds are dead."

"Perks of this job, I tell you," she said, pulling up her phone and frowning. "There has been little to no traction on the Davidsons since the Fitzgeralds news broke. That blows my mind. I know the media is biased but—"

"Could be intentional leaks. Someone doesn't want the truth getting out, so they give hot topic information. Churchgoers get killed? That sparks outcry. Former drug dealer? Not as much. Alright, we're here."

Cooper pulled into the parking lot of the local precinct. He exited the SUV and waited for Addyson before walking behind her. She had a spine of steel when she wanted, and he admired her for putting away her charming personality for the case. It took discipline to do that well. Another wave of pride went through him.

"We're here to see Fisher," she held up her badge and kept her face blank when the woman paged someone in the back. The door clicked, and a young woman with large glasses called for them to follow her through two large doors.

"Mr. Fisher is busy, but he'll be out soon." She walked away, her heels clicking on the tile. They didn't have to wait more than a minute before the door opened, leaving them face-to-face with the leader of the Vampire Roman Clan, Reginald.

5

"The man I once knew as Addison. You go by Cooper, no?" Reginald Roman held out his arms and pulled Cooper into an awkward embrace. The vampire was tall and thin where Cooper was muscle and girth. The men hugged, and Addyson fought the urge to question what the vampire said.

Addison? Interesting.

"Reggie, it is always a pleasure to see you. I take it you're being proactive for your clan with all this going on?" Cooper asked, continuing to keep a hand on the vampire's shoulder.

"You know me well. Yes. Humans cannot wait to pin this sort of thing on us despite the fact we leave evidence. Are there bite marks? No. Did they lose blood? No. Are there reporters around our residence, accusing us of the crime? Yes. It is madness."

Fisher looked between the two men, and Addy studied him. His mind raced so fast she barely caught on to his channel. Fear, worry, and betrayal leaked out of him, and her heart rate picked up with the thrill of the chase. "Y-you two know each other?"

"Yes, we go back." Reginald smiled at Fisher before directing his attention to Addyson. Her veins chilled at the sight of him—a natural reaction when a vampire laid eyes on someone with blood. It didn't matter how many decades went on with regulations—the body knew when a hunter neared them. "Ah, who is this luscious creature?"

"This is Addy," Cooper said, moving to put his hand on her lower back. "Addyson."

"Ah, *your* Addyson?"

She threw Cooper a confused look, and the tips of his cheeks turned pink. "We are partnering on this case together, hoping to get it solved as quickly as we can. The SSS doesn't need to spend more resources on human and paranormal relations."

"True. Very true." Reginald held out a hand, and she shook it, noting how he was warm to the touch. "You are a beauty, Addyson. Cooper spoke highly of you."

"He spoke highly of you, too, Reginald."

"Reggie, dear. Please. Reginald is my father, and I refuse to use that name unless as a power play." He made a face of disgust and brought the back of her hand to his mouth. He pressed a light kiss there and hummed in delight. "You, too, have a gift. Interesting. This new wave of paras is distracting because you do not have features that are noticeable."

"But you can tell from a handshake?" she asked, curious as to how he'd known immediately.

"I can smell it in your blood, dear." He patted her hand before giving it back to her. "I need to leave, but I can rest easier knowing you will clear this, Cooper. If you get any time off, you are always welcome to visit. Bring your Addyson with you."

Cooper shook his hand again and met her gaze, the warmth radiating from him enough to almost distract her from the issue at hand: solving murders. "See you soon, Reggie."

The vampire smiled and walked swiftly out of sight. Just as the door to the main area shut, Fisher walked through looking rough. He approached quietly and Cooper gave him his attention. "Fisher."

"C-come to my office, please." The man wreaked of weakness,

and Addyson didn't want to touch anything in his gross office. Wrappers lined the floor, and old coffee mugs on the side table contained mold. Fisher sat behind his desk and blinked so often Addy itched her own eye to make sure hers were fine. "You have questions about the Davidsons?"

"Yes, Detective Braxton wants to ask you a few things," she answered, hoping he would get the hint. If Cooper asked, she would be free to pry into Fisher's mind. Doing both at the same time posed a challenge. She'd be up for it, but if Cooper could take the lead, it'd be easier. Her skin prickled with a hint of something heavy, and she wanted full access to him.

"Go ahead." He crossed his arms and leaned onto the desktop. She'd assumed he'd welcome their questions, but unease and nerves radiated off him. Sweat beaded all along his brow, and his dilated pupils gave him a disturbing appearance. "Ask away."

"Tell us about how the Davidsons were reported missing. Who did you talk to?"

"Well, uh... The daughter, Kayla, didn't show up to work at the restaurant..." He trailed off and Addyson masked her face as she tried to see inside his mind. He'd gone to the restaurant and interviewed the manager. The girl hadn't shown up three days in a row and missed picking up her paycheck—a first for her. The manager thought it suspicious because she'd needed money. He'd called the house and her emergency contact and never received an answer. After a few more days, he'd tried again and finally notified the police.

She blinked herself out of his memories.

"Did you go visit their place yourself?" she asked, interrupting Cooper's line of questioning. He didn't seem to mind. His eyes warmed at her, and she wondered if he could see the glow in hers as she worked her powers.

"Y-yes. There were signs of struggle. Drugs everywhere." She made a face at Cooper, and he kept talking to the guy as she dug into his memory again. The weathered house looked rough with the chipped siding and rusted windows. But someone took care of it. Someone had cleaned the inside recently, it seemed. The carpet showed vacuum lines and scents of lemon soap filled the air. The only thing out of place was white powder on the coffee table, the counter, and the floor. Seemed too inconsistent with drug use. It seemed staged.

Cooper leaned back into his chair and ran his hand over his impeccable jawline. "What did you do after visiting the house?"

"Went to the parents' places of work to see if they knew anything. They didn't. I tried a couple more times until I spoke to their supervisor. He hadn't seen them either. Said they'd just stopped showing up one day and he didn't have time or energy to look into it."

"The neighbors witness anything?"

"Nope. They weren't sad to see them go, to be honest." Fisher grabbed a tissue and wiped his brow before tossing it into the trash can. "No one heard or saw anything."

Addyson listened to his smarmy voice and replayed what she could from his mind. Something needed to bring attention to this case. "Did you talk to their parole officers?"

He paled. "Y-yes. They said the Davidsons were lost causes."

"Why are you scared, Fisher?" Cooper asked, not raising his voice but changing the tone to almost assertive. It caused Addyson to sit up straighter, and she noted the change in Fisher too.

His eyes widened and his fingers trembled before he fisted his hands.

"You're stuttering and answering questions like someone is watching you," Cooper said.

"No. I'm not scared. Nothing like that, no." Fisher blinked too fast and crossed his arms, then uncrossed them. Sat back in the chair, then leaned forward. Too much movement. Too awkward.

He's lying.

"You can say 'no' all you want, Fisher, but you're giving yourself away. Are you safe?" Cooper asked, standing up and searching the room. "Is there a camera in here or something?"

Fisher crumpled his face into an almost pout before he swallowed hard. "No. There's not."

He widened his eyes at Addyson, jerking his head toward the side of his desk. "No cameras at all. What a weird question."

Addyson frowned as Fisher kept moving his gaze to the pen holder. A muscle in his cheek twitched, and Cooper picked up on the hint.

Cooper nudged the cup filled with pens, knocked it on the ground, then stomped his boot on the device. "I'm sure we don't have much time. Now, what the fuck is going on?"

"Someone told me to stay away from this case, okay? No one wants to spend money or resources on a bunch of lowlives."

"Who directed you to do this?" Cooper asked the million-dollar question. "Hansen?"

"No way. He's too straight." Fisher wiped his face and looked on the verge of tears. "It goes beyond the station."

Addyson took a deep breath, and her veins vibrated as she felt the truth leave him. *Someone had threatened him. This Nate character. He's holding Fisher's daughter captive until the case is forgotten. If he tells anyone, she'll die.*

She stilled and tried to figure out how to deal with the situation. It was difficult enough trying to guess why the Fitzgeralds had been killed, but to know a young girl was now caught in the middle of it... Her heart ached. "Fisher," she said, the tone and aggression making her sound nothing like herself. "Can you reach out to him?"

"W-what do you mean?"

"Do you have a way of contacting him?"

He blinked faster, and water leaked out of the corner of his eyes. "Yes."

"Cooper is going to punch you in the face, and I'm going to cut your neck—nothing serious, but it will bleed. You are going to call Nate and tell him we knocked you out, but you gave nothing away."

"How do you... They'll kill my daughter!"

"I know. That's why you're going to call him right now. It's been about three minutes since the camera broke, and he's either on his way here or going to her." She stood and took a knife out from her ankle brace. "Come here."

He shook and trembled to the point he threw up into the trash can. "She's all I have."

"We will do whatever we can to get her back, but if you don't do this, your daughter could be in even more danger." She jutted her chin up to have him copy the gesture. He did, his entire body jerking. "Okay, this will just be a surface wound."

Cooper placed a hand over hers and stopped. "I can do it. Keep guard."

She understood his instructions. *Listen to their minds.* She stood by the door and aimlessly scrolled through the others in the building. Their thoughts about dinner plans, corruption in politics, and...*he's here.* "Cooper."

He finished slicing his neck and pocketed the knife, looking in her direction. "Is it him?"

"Yes." Her eyes widened, and her pulse speed up when she felt his power. He oozed authority and cruelty. Often, she sensed people's dirtiest thoughts, and his were worse. He would do whatever it took to get what he wanted. That, she knew for certain. "He's marching this way now."

Cooper didn't show any fear when he blinked and lowered his voice. "Follow my lead."

Fisher wept, the blood dripping to his shirt. Cooper snapped his fingers. "Fisher, pull your shit together."

"Think of Julia. Do this for her." She moved to sit back down, but Cooper picked her up and set her on the other side of the desk. He put a finger to his lips before punching Fisher square in the face as the door burst open and the Chief of Police, Nathanial Castro, walked in.

"What in the hell is going on?" he barked, his eyes scanning the room and landing briefly on the shattered camera. His hand went to his gun on his side, and Cooper held his arms in the air.

"Arrest me if you must, Chief. But Fisher hit on my fucking girlfriend after I told him explicitly to shut the hell up." Cooper pretended to hit him again, and Fisher flinched like they'd rehearsed it. Blood dripped from his nose and the poor guy whimpered.

"Fisher. Is this true?"

He nodded and reached for tissues to stop the bleeding. Addyson handed him the box before glaring at Cooper. "You are such an asshole."

"I protect what's mine."

"I'm not a delicate flower, Braxton." She made her voice fluctuate and gave the Chief a sheepish smile. "This is more than embarrassing."

"We have a strict policy about partners fucking here. I know things are different at the SSS." He sneered and turned up his nose, making his opinion on paranormals quite clear. "Why are you here?"

"I'm sure you heard about the Fitzgeralds and Davidsons. Our agency wanted us to take a look since it could involve paranormals." Cooper wiped his hand on the side of his pants and held it out. "Nice to meet you, Chief. Braxton, Cooper Braxton."

The extremely large man with dark facial hair and tiny eyes shook Cooper's hand before reaching out to Addy's. "Sorry you saw that, sir," she said. The Chief let his eyes drag over her face then to her chest for a few seconds before breaking into a smile. Cooper growled under his breath, but the Chief didn't seem to care.

"Kinda thought Fisher a weasel without a backbone, but I commend you, Fisher, for going for it."

The man nodded but continued to look at the ground. Cooper remained between Nate and Addyson, pointing to the camera. "I found a monitoring device, sir. Not sure how long or for what, but I smashed it. Your techs might want to take a look."

The Chief's gaze narrowed slightly before he nodded. "Thank you. I'll bring it to them. Now, why don't we head into my office? I'll provide any information you want on the Davidsons."

"No need. Fisher was a dead end," Addyson said, plastering on her sweet smile that melted the hardest criminals. Her veins hummed when she moved closer to the Chief, but it wasn't with warmth. It felt cool, almost like an impenetrable wall of water. "We were hoping to find a path between them and paranormals. There's a turf war going on with the vamps and wolves right now, and any human collateral would rule in the opposition's favor."

His eyes lit up. "Interesting. Did you know about this, Fisher?"

"No," Cooper barged in. "It is our job to know the politics of paranormals. We wanted to get information before sharing our bias. We're thinking the daughter ran into the wrong crowd at the restaurant. Met a guy, stole drugs, that sort of thing."

"Ah, yes. Kayla was always a bit wild for this town."

"We have to report back to our boss, but we'll reach out if we need more information." Cooper pretended to hit Fisher again. "You have nice taste man, but stay away from my woman."

"Y-yes sir," he mumbled before looking at Addyson. "I'm sorry for h-hitting on you."

She shrugged. "I'd say no harm, no foul, but Cooper is a possessive asshole." She rolled her eyes and smiled at the Chief again. "Have a good night."

"You, too, doll."

Addyson felt his gaze all over her as she walked down the narrow hallway and back through the entrance. Instead of heading to the car, Cooper led them down the block with his hand on her lower back. She started to talk, but he silenced her with a soft hiss. They walked in the heat for another ten minutes before he pulled them into a bar. The dim lights and aimless chatter drowned out the worry in her head. She tried to speak again, and he gave her a look. He pulled out his phone and called for an Uber.

It didn't take long, and he never stopped touching her. They waited in the dingy bar, his hand on the base of her back, and she felt each time he breathed. His lips were close to her ear, and she swore he brushed them against her temple as they waited in silence. Once the Uber arrived, they went to the nearest hotel.

"Room for one night, please," he said, not taking his hand off her. When she attempted to move away, he held on to her belt loop. After three attempts, she decided to stay close to him. She tried to read his mind but couldn't get through and relied on normal senses. His voice tensed and his muscles remained stiff. The easy smile had been replaced with intense focus, and when they gave him a key for a room on the top floor, he took her hand and led her into the elevator. Once they'd reached the room, he waited until he'd finished searching it for bugs before he spoke again.

"Nate is a paranormal." He clenched his fist to his side and yelled out a string of curse words. "He's a fucking paranormal parading like a human."

"I know." She sat on the edge of the bed, fell onto her back, and stared at the weak ceiling fan barely stirring the air. It was a huge leap, but she decided she did trust Cooper. At least with her life. Maybe not her heart. The time had come to clear the question hanging between them. "Seeing memories is what I do. I read their emotions and can plug in to whatever thought is in their mind. I can't do it with other paranormals, though. Nate's mind was a wall."

She closed her eyes and waited eight beats before sitting up and searching Cooper's face for a reaction. She'd never explained her powers to anyone besides her bosses. It felt...intimate to share it with Cooper, a former lover. Even though he was a paranormal, too, it exposed a part of herself that society didn't like. She'd finally told him after all this time, and he went radio silent? Anger flushed her skin, and she gritted her teeth. "I tell you that and you say nothing? Are you kidding me?"

"Addy," he said, moving from the small table to position himself between her legs. He kneeled down so they were eye to eye and cupped the back of her neck with his hand. His face looked so pained, like he longed for her, and she didn't stop him when he traced her bottom lip with his thumb. She trembled with need. "You trust me," he said.

She nibbled on his thumb, and he groaned, resting his forehead against hers as his breathing picked up. Her own heart pounded against her ribcage. She panted and ran her fingers through his hair again. She pulled it so his face pointed at hers again. "With my life, yes."

"What about your heart?" he asked, pressing a kiss to her breastbone, just above her heart.

She couldn't trust her voice. Not when he moved his mouth up to her neck, dropping kiss after kiss on her skin. He took a deep breath and sighed against her, sending ripples of goose bumps down her body. "Addy, my god."

She squirmed when he dragged his teeth down her neck and her traitorous nipples pebbled beneath her bra. She willed them to settle down before he saw. They were one of his favorite features, if she remembered correctly. "Coop..." Her voice shook, and he pulled back with such a tender look on his face she almost broke down and begged him to kiss her. "What are you doing?"

"I missed your skin. Your smell. Your fucking hair." He dipped low and sucked on her earlobe while he moved his hands down her back. He cradled her against him, pulling her tight so there wasn't any space between their chests. She missed his warmth so damn badly. It physically hurt to be this close to him and to remember the heartache.

"Your sounds and your smile and your heart," he continued.

She closed her eyes and let herself enjoy the feel of his lips on her. A little kiss here and there wouldn't be terrible. She could enjoy it without getting hurt again. He took his time with each move, and she swore his body shook when she ran her hands over his strong shoulders and back. She whimpered when he massaged down her neck to her collarbone, pulling the skin with his teeth before sucking it into his warmth mouth. He made no attempt to undo her shirt, and after minutes of squirming beneath him, she arched her hips against him. She *wanted* him, even though she knew it'd be dangerous.

"Baby," his voice came out strained. "I'm trying to wait for you to kiss me, but I'm dying. Can I see you? Touch you?"

She wanted to say yes, but her heart stopped her. "Cooper," she said, the warning in her voice clear for both of them. "I—"

Someone pounded on the door and they both jumped.

"It's Hansen. Open up if you want to live."

6

THE OLDER MAN PLOPPED HIMSELF DOWN ON THE WOODEN CHAIR near the patio, and Cooper made himself a goddamn drink. His dick throbbed, and Addyson wouldn't look at him. Throw in a corrupt police chief, a girl being held hostage, and a death threat, and he'd had himself the weirdest day of his career.

"I can't stay long, but this town is small. People talk."

"Why are you here?" Addyson asked with a slight tremor in her voice. Cooper wanted to credit himself for why she looked flustered but figured it could also be the situation they were in. Who was to say?

"Chief put out word that paranormals were trying to undermine our guys. Really set the tone against you, and some take offense to the paras stealing our jobs."

"Then why be dramatic about it?" she asked, making an annoyed face. "Anytime we intervene in any investigation, people get pissed. This isn't news, nor does it bother us."

Good. She's feisty. Cooper loved when Addy went all badass on others.

Hansen paled and pinched the bridge of his nose. "He has guys following you. I respect you both and felt the need to tell you. There's a tracker on your car, and he has spies all over town. Knows you're here. He's done some shady shit in the past, and whenever he watches someone, it doesn't end well for them."

"Is this a warning or a threat?" Cooper asked, moving to sit on the other chair. "Why risk being seen or getting caught? Unless you're here as a distraction?"

A blank look clouded Addyson's face, and her hazel eyes brightened before she smiled. "He admired my balls and your track record. I believe Hansen is here out of respect."

"The lady is right." He nervously looked out the window. "Chief isn't happy you know Reginald Roman."

Addyson chimed in. "He tried to pin this all on his clan, but Reggie is smarter than your chief and made sure to prevent the lie from spreading. Reggie made himself quite clear at the station —he will protect the Romani name."

Cooper admired the fuck out of this woman and still couldn't believe he'd let her go. Not that he needed more motivation to win her back, but seeing her in her element did things to him. He beamed with pride at her when Hansen nodded and lost color in his face. "Right you are, again."

"Thanks for letting us know. We'll plan accordingly." Cooper stood and wanted to walk the man out, but Hansen paused when Addyson spoke up again.

"Keep an eye out for Fisher. He's a pawn in a larger game."

"That kid? Heard he got what he deserved." His eyes traveled to Cooper, and he gave him a nod. "He was always too slimy for my liking."

"It's not his fault. Have you seen Addy? Anyone would hit on her," Cooper said, not caring that he sounded like a lovestruck idiot. Addyson furrowed her brows for a beat before a slight blush covered her neck. Then he clapped Hansen on the back. "Look out for the kid."

"Will do. Watch your backs and let me know if I can help in any way, alright?"

Cooper led him to the door and paused before leaning against it, then stared at Addyson. "What were you going to say before he knocked?"

"What?" She blushed and crossed her arms over her chest.

"You said, 'I,' before he interrupted." He stalked toward her and lifted her chin with a gentle tilt. Her breathing picked up and he liked it. "I was doing this." He kissed her neck again, slowly, dragging his tongue just under her ear. "And you said…"

"You chose Addison as your undercover name."

He pulled back and met her eyes. "Yes."

"Why?"

"Because whenever I let myself forget who I was, your name brought me back—every time I heard it."

Her eyelids fluttered, and she pressed her lips together before opening up those gorgeous hazel eyes that couldn't hide any emotions. "What's your power?"

"I project thoughts onto others to get them to do things."

"You've never…done that to me?"

"Are you kidding?" He laughed. "I never would. Not to you."

"Can you…try?"

He swallowed, nerves dancing along his spine. This was his fear—that he'd *projected* her feelings for him back then, before he left. That he'd clouded her judgement of being with him. "Sure."

Doing the thing he'd never dared to do, he let his power radiate from him and pushed *hug me* toward Addy. No zing or hum happened. He tried again, then stumbled back in proud relief. It didn't work.

"Did you try?" she asked, her voice small.

"Yes." He grinned so hard his face hurt. "It doesn't work. For so long, I've worried I'd projected feelings onto you, never knowing if you'd felt the same way." He cupped her face. "Now I know."

She licked her lower lip as he leaned closer. "Why did you leave me?"

"Because I found out I was a paranormal, and it scared the shit out of me." He pushed a lock of her hair behind her ear, and she rested the side of her face on his palm. That simple gesture made his entire body tingle with pleasure. "I didn't know what my powers could do, and I didn't want to subject you to that life. There were still prejudices against paras, and you could've been targeted, hurt, harassed... I left to protect you."

She squeezed her eyes together, and when she opened them, a sadness ran deep. "You made the decision without talking to me."

"It is the thing I regret most in my entire life." His voice shook and he went for it. *All or nothing.* "I found out you were a para a year after I left, but you were in the beginning of your career, kicking ass. I watched and became patient. I figured you would never give me the time of day if I just strolled into your life again, so I waited until an opportunity presented itself. My job gave me joy, and when I learned we paired up with other agencies from time to time, I asked my boss to let me know when your branch of SSS needed some extra help."

"What if that chance never happened?"

"But it did," he said softly, moving closer to her. "It did, and I'm here, and I want to kiss you."

"Want me to kiss the truth out of you, huh?" she teased, and he hoped she would forgive him. Maybe not now, but someday.

"Ask me any goddamn thing you want, but please, I want to taste you, Addyson. I need it." His entire body shook with desire and anticipation. She closed the distance between them, then ran her hands over his chest and moved to cup his face.

"First, truth. What do you envision our future being if I give in to this? Give in to you?"

"Kiss, and I'll tell you."

She hummed and brought her lips to his in a quick peck. She tried to lean away, but he pulled her against him, lifting her and wrapping her legs around him as he kneaded his fingers into her ass. "Nope," he demanded, bringing her mouth to his so he could finally fucking taste her. Her pillow lips were soft and willing. She kissed like she held the air in his lungs and groaned when he bit down on her lip and sucked it.

"Coop," she moaned and opened her mouth to let him explore more. She tasted like mint and smelled like a combination of sweat and lotion. She deepened the embrace and tightened her grip in his hair, and he swore his knees wobbled.

He dropped her to the bed but remained on top of her, moving to trail kisses along her neckline. "I fucking missed you."

"I missed you too," she said, her voice full of lust and want. It drove him wild, and he kissed her harder. Her mouth, her neck, her ear, her nose, her forehead. He couldn't get enough of her soft skin. "The investigation."

"What about it?" he asked, repositioning himself so he could unbutton her white shirt. He undid three before her lacy, beige bra teased him. He paused and bit down on his fist. "Christ, your body..."

Her entire face reddened, and a small smile played on her lips. "We should do something."

"I am doing something." He finished with her shirt, took it off, and tossed it to the side. He couldn't stop from staring. Her body defined perfection. Smooth and curvy, but still strong. She had a birth mark right above her belly button and he bent down and kissed it. "I'm getting my fill of you."

"But the case," she said, her breath getting heavier when he trailed kisses up her middle, between her breasts. "We should...should..."

He pulled her bra cups down and took one pebbled nipple into his mouth. He moaned as he cupped each breast, teasing and swirling his tongue around the tip. She arched her back, and he moved to the other breast, repeating the process and then blowing on them. The dusty pink points looked like gum drops. He traced the outline of one with his finger as he flicked the other with his tongue, and Addyson's chest moved up and down as she panted. "Cooper, my god."

"You like this, Ads?" He repeated the process until she squirmed on the bed. "If I reached between your legs, would you be wet for me?"

"Yes," she said, her teeth clenching as he spent more time on her breasts. They'd always been her favorite form of foreplay, and he could spend hours pleasing her. He was a boob guy through and through, and her tits were amazing.

"Reach down and undo your belt," he demanded, not stopping the sensational teasing around her nipples. She obeyed. He scooted to the side. "Remove your panties."

She did.

Soft curls covered her mound, and he groaned at the sight of her spread thighs. He released one nipple with a loud pop and moved down her body. A desperate, carnal urge took over. He nipped the skin below her belly button, sucking it lightly before going lower. He wanted to bury his face in her pussy. Make her scream with pleasure as he ate her for hours. "Cooper, you don't... You don't have to—"

"But baby, I need to." He did. He really fucking did.

He pushed her legs farther and licked her, taking in her scent and almost exploding in his pants at how wet she was for him. He flicked his tongue in and out, swirling around her swollen clit and bringing her close to the edge before backing off. She squirmed on the bed, thrashing her head back and forth as he changed pace. Her muscular thighs clenched, and sweat pooled on her stomach. He loved her naked and open for him like this. She was a fucking dream, and he took his time, flattening his tongue against her, nice and slow. She shuddered like he wanted her to, and he stopped. "Addy," he said before gently biting the inside of her thigh. "Do you still have feelings for me?"

"Cooper," her voice went dangerously low, and he smiled.

"Truth or kiss, baby." He sucked her clit back into his mouth, and her legs shook violently around him. She was close—oh so close. Her chest heaved, and her moans got louder and louder. Lifting his head, he asked, "Do you think about me when you touch yourself?"

"Stop teasing me."

"Answer then." He loved her feisty attitude and take-no-shit tone. It was foreplay for him. He slid one finger, then two into her and slowly thrusted in and out. She trembled and gripped his shoulders.

"Please."

She let out a groan and reached her hand down to stimulate herself. She used her fingers to put pressure on her clit, and Cooper forgot how to breathe. *Holy shit.* He craved to see her do that, but right now, her pleasure belonged to him. He wanted to taste when she fell apart. It had been too long without being with her, and he planned to taste every single drop. He flicked her hand away and brought his mouth back to her center. "Addy."

"Yes!" she screamed as he quickened the pace, placing a hand on her stomach to steady her as she convulsed around him. Her orgasms had always been long and aggressive. They didn't last only a few seconds—they were almost a minute of pure ecstasy. Her entire body shook, and sweat glistened on her skin by the time she came down. He ate up every ounce of her pleasure and pressed one final kiss to her before glancing up at her.

She was fucking beautiful and bare. Natural and strong.

He helped her slide her panties back on and fixed her bra in place before he put his weight on his elbows and looked down at her. Her eyes were unfocused, and he grinned. "You're incredible."

"You went down on me."

"Yes, I did. I'll do it every goddamn day if you want it." He kissed her nose and tried reading her post-orgasm expression. Her eyes were hooded, and she looked worried. "If you say you regret it, you will break my heart."

"No, that's not it." Her face softened, and she blinked a couple of times. "It's been so long since someone did that to me, I forgot how...intense it can be."

"Addyson, placate me and let me pretend there hasn't been anyone else. I cannot fathom you sharing this with another man." He sat up and ignored his throbbing dick. He would have to wait. This was about her. *Maybe we can fool around later.*

She laughed. "There is no way you haven't slept with numerous women since we split."

"Are we doing this?"

"You brought it up." She shrugged and started putting her shirt back on. "Wait." She gestured to the bulge in his pants. "What about you?"

"Despite the blood loss to my entire body, I can wait." He stood and stretched, not bothering to hide his evident reaction. "I want to sink into you for hours, Ads. I want to spend an entire week in bed with you, and this hotel room is not the place."

"But," she said, frowning. "You got me off."

"I wanted you to remember how good we are together." He moved toward her again and started buttoning her shirt. "I projected Hansen to tell Fisher to meet us at that shady bar we passed earlier—in fifteen minutes. If I get to slide into your pussy, baby, I need more time than that."

"That's what you think," she quipped back, and he burst out laughing. She chuckled, too, and the air between them settled. Once her clothes were in place and his wood went back to a regular size, a thoughtful look crossed her face. "I *do* still have feelings for you. They are messy and we have a lot to talk about."

He took his first real breath and felt a million pounds lighter. "We can talk, or not talk, for as long as you want."

She smiled and patted his face. "I felt guilty about not helping Fisher and his daughter. You arranged for him to meet us to get more information, huh?"

"Right. I don't play nice with men who use children as leverage. When they fuck with me, they end up losing something." He felt the anger ebb and flow.

"What types of things?" She intertwined their fingers as they left the room. It was such a simple action, it made no sense his entire heart amped up.

"Money or body parts."

She snorted and leaned her head on his shoulder for a second. "To answer your previous question, I did think about you when I touched myself these past couple years. You're soft but such a badass and selfless in bed. There haven't been many men in my life, and not one of them compares to you. Not even a close second place."

He kissed the back of her hand. "Good. I plan to keep it that way for a long time."

They headed to the bar, and despite the dangerous situation they were bound to walk into, he felt better, hopeful even. She still held feelings for him. He was smitten. Stupidly smitten. Which was the only reason he didn't see a man running full speed at them. He'd barely pushed Addy behind him by the time the hit came—like a goddamn bull. He flew into the air and landed on his back. Intense pain blasted through his body when his head smacked the concrete.

Another one came. And a third.

Addy's voice sounded like she was inside a distorted radio. He blinked, looking up at the sun, and it blurred as if sizzling. *That's not good.* He closed his eyes and welcomed the blackness that came over him. It was easier than dealing with the weight repeatedly landing on his chest.

7

THE WILDLING MOVED FAST, BUT ADDYSON HAD TRAINED FOR HIS. Cooper shoved her behind him, which was heroic, but also idiotic. It gave the guy full access to his chest, and he landed too many punches on him for her liking. She took two large steps to gain momentum before jumping into the air. She landed a swift kick to the guy's neck, fell to the ground, and propped herself back up onto her feet for another round.

"What the fuck do you want?" she asked, throwing a punch at his kidney when he turned around to shield himself. He groaned and fell to his knees. She shoved him onto the asphalt and pressed her foot to his neck. Cooper remained on the ground, unmoving, but she couldn't let herself worry about him until she restrained this guy. "Who are you?"

"Mitch," he mumbled when she put pressure on her foot. "Someone hired me to mug you."

"Why?"

He remained silent and she pressed harder. "I asked you a question. It'd be wise to answer."

His mind hadn't given her any hint as to the why or who yet;

she needed to prompt his memories to get more information. "Mitch, tell me what I want."

"Listen to her, man," Cooper said, his voice strained.

Mitch groaned and Addy shifted her weight, causing Mitch more pain. He finally broke and cried out. "I got cash, lady. Damn."

"Who hired you?"

The man's voice broke. "I don't know! Fuck. I'd never seen him before."

Bingo. She entered his thoughts and searched back to the memory of him getting paid. Clear as day, she saw the Chief. He wore street clothes and a hat, his appearance making him seem like a casual, everyday citizen. She pressed a little harder on him and waited for whatever he held dear to cross his mind. Mitch had a son. "If I let you go, which I don't have to do, what will you do?"

"Not say a word. I'll hide, I swear." He started crying, and she released her foot from him. He glanced up, tears and snot dripping down his face, and he looked down the street. "You lettin' me leave?"

Her favorite part of her abilities was this—figuring out what made people tick. Sometimes, she used it to her advantage, but others...she helped them help themselves. Mitch had fucked up, but people did all sorts of things to protect their own.

"You go *straight* to your son and stay the fuck away from the man who paid you. You understand? He's not as nice as I am. And if you make me regret this, I will personally see that you don't have any more kids, you feel me?"

He nodded and took off running, and only then did she kneel to the ground and cover Cooper's face with her hand. "Coop? God, tell me you're okay."

"That was fucking hot, Ads. I don't remember you being that badass," he mumbled, wincing when he tried opening his eyes. "You scared the fucker."

"I'm good at what I do. I told you." She blocked the sun and commanded him to follow her finger with his eyes. "You have a concussion."

"Shit. Figured as much." He pushed himself to sit up, and the bruise and swelling had already formed around his eye. She reached out and touched it, and he captured her hand. "I've never been protected before."

She smiled. "How did it feel?"

"I like knowing you have my back. We're a good pair, you and me. I'd like to team up with you for everything. Work, life, grocery shopping..."

"How hard did he hit your head?" Her body zinged with the weight of his words, but she attributed it to the concussion. "I can't imagine grocery shopping being this eventful."

"Oh, it can. I need you there."

Her lips twitched. Even though the injury looked bad, his humor remained. She'd always enjoyed his quick wit and jokes. They were a contrast to her seriousness, and seeing him bruised, on the ground, did something to her. Made her insides get all tight and twisted. "Let me help you up."

"Woman, allow me to have some dignity." He groaned and took his time, but he stood and put an arm around her neck for balance. "Alright. Let's head inside."

"You want to... Are you kidding me? No. We need to go to the hospital."

"Later. We have a timeline to catch this guy, and I think the Davidsons are still alive. They've been gone for three weeks, and if the Fitzgeralds were a distraction, why haven't they been found dead? He's keeping them." He took a moment and rubbed his forehead. "Fisher's daughter can't wait for me to sit out for a few hours." He closed his eyes and slowed their walk. "A dark bar and a beer sound great."

"You aren't drinking," she scoffed, rolling her eyes at his

audacity. Per usual, Cooper refused to acknowledge his limits. "Dark bar, fine, but no beer."

A goofy smile covered his face, and he nuzzled her neck. "I like it when you boss me."

"You say that now. In a month, you'll be sick of it."

"A month, you say? You'll be with me in a month?" His voice sounded hopeful and adorable, and her heart skipped a beat. She felt breathless.

"Maybe. I'll think about it."

"Alls I ask, baby. Don't say no. It'll gut me." He slurred his words, and worry took root in her gut. It did no one good for him to be out for the count. She guided them to the bar and shoved him inside with one more look down the road. She couldn't say how or why, but she felt someone watching them. For shits and giggles, she put her middle finger into the air before joining Cooper in the dive. He staggered to a booth where Fisher sat, mouth agape and even paler than before, and Addyson slid in, offering a smile.

"You okay, Fisher? Any word on your daughter?"

"No." He grimaced and took a loud sip of his water. "Nate believed you earlier. I couldn't... It was insane, but it worked."

"Good," Cooper said, rubbing the spot between his eyes. "The fucker sent someone to attack me. Means you were probably followed here."

"Shit! They can't. No!"

"They didn't follow you," Addyson said. "They hired him to find us at the hotel. Purely coincidence he found us outside this place."

"Are you sure?"

"Yes. One perk of being a paranormal is I can spot lies. Trust me on this, alright?"

Fisher tried to smile, but it came out like a cry. She continued. "Okay, details. Where did he take your daughter? When? The

Davidsons were reported missing three weeks ago. It's been that long?"

"Yes." His hands shook. "He lets me video chat her every night. He's there with her, doing God knows what, but he's always in the background. Thirty minutes. Eight-thirty."

She nodded, her blood humming with the thrill of the chase. It didn't matter what type of creature they were dealing with, taking a *child* broke every code in the book, and she wanted revenge. Craved it, actually. Her mind raced, but she kept her face and pulse in check. "Good. We can work with this information."

"You-you're going to help me get her back?" Fisher swallowed hard, hope billowing in his eyes. That spark of hope drove her motivation even further. Addy wouldn't rest until they found his daughter.

"Fuck yeah, we are." Cooper leveled his gaze with Fisher, and Addy would've smiled at his furrowed brows if the situation wasn't so vile. "I think the Davidsons are there, too. I think— Damn, my brain hurts... If you get your daughter back, we find out the truth about the Davidsons."

Fisher broke down into tears and repeated his gratitude over and over. "How? How will we do this?"

"The call." Addyson snapped her fingers. "We'll set up a screen so we can see the call. He won't know, and we can search for clues. Possibly track it even."

"He told me if I track it, I won't see her again," he said, his lips trembling. "He'll know."

"No. That's a lie. He won't know, Fisher." She tried to assure him, but it only seemed to fluster him more. Those blanket threats worked on those who had something to lose.

Cooper cleared his throat and moved closer to Addy, resting a hand on her thigh under the table. "Dude, take a breath. This is a lot, but we don't fuck up. We'll get your girl. We have what...a couple hours to get set up? Let's get moving."

"Sure, but I don't think you're telling me everything you

learned about the Davidsons." Addy narrowed her gaze at Fisher.

The man's eyes turned to saucers, and large beads of sweat fell down his temples. "I shared all I know! I swear!"

"Sorry, I meant your *memories* hold more information than you recalled. I'd... I'd like to see them."

He blinked and held out his hands like she could read palms. She snorted and shook her head. "Cute, but no. I need you to think about the case again. Every detail."

"And this will help?"

"Yes." She leaned onto her elbows. "Go through every interview, photograph, call, conversation, and memory you have. Cooper's right. I have a feeling the Davidsons are connected to this, and once we figure that out, we can make our plan."

"Sure. Okay. Yeah." Fisher closed his eyes tightly, and she relaxed, diving into the vibrant memories from the past three weeks. Nothing jumped out. She sifted through the questioning, him speaking to the neighbors, images of the restaurant where the daughter worked, and the strange fact no one missed them. There were bouts of his extreme worry and sadness laced into every conversation, and her heart ached for him.

She watched a scene replay of him talking to the restaurant manager. There was a back room with a one-way door. Windowless. No handle. A keypad. That seemed...odd. No restaurant she'd been to had contained that type of security on a door. She withdrew herself. "Is that restaurant known for anything scandalous?"

His face blushed. "It has certain clientele."

"Talk, man. My head is killing me." Cooper rubbed his temples and groaned.

Fisher winced and wiped a hand over his face. "Okay, there is a club in the back for members. They pay a certain fee and enjoy...women entertainers."

"And the Davidson daughter entertained...guests?"

"No one confirmed or denied this. She waitressed in the front often, so it was assumed she didn't work in the back."

"Never assume, man. Never. Tell me, does your Chief go there often?" Cooper asked.

Somehow, his milky skin turned whiter. "Y-yes. He did."

"Have you ever seen them together in the same room?"

His face twisted in disgust and told her all she needed to know. Addy saw what he remembered: the Chief touching the daughter's thigh as she walked by, her sitting on his lap with a crowd of people around them, and in every memory, she wore little clothing.

"And it took the police three days to search the house with the fake, planted drugs?

"Yes."

Addyson relaxed into the booth and held up her fingers. "Whatever she did, heard, saw, or was involved in, that's the key."

"How do we find her?" Fisher asked, blinking faster by the second. "He has my daughter. She is my life."

"I know." Addy softened her voice and started forming a plan in her mind. "We'll call some people who can work their tech magic. Does he call from a cellphone or a computer?"

"Not sure. She's normally sitting on a chair talking to me." He ran shaky hands through his hair before wiping his sweaty brow. "Must be a computer, now that I think about it. Nate is always in the background."

"Perfect." She texted what they needed to Patricio, under-lining the fact this could not be relayed to the local police. "Alright, my boss is sending our best guy. Should be here in a couple hours. Lines up perfectly with your phone call time."

"Do we just sit here and wait?" He eyed his watch.

"You go back to work and act normal since it's only four-thirty. You will be followed if they haven't already trailed you here. We'll sneak out the back and proceed like normal—interview her place of work, talk to Fitzgerald's neighbors, that sort of thing. Write your address down on the napkin. We'll meet there at seven."

"Normal. Act normal. Okay. I can do that."

"Good. Now go. You've been here too long." She jutted her chin. "Go."

Fisher left them at the booth, and Cooper rested his forehead on her shoulder as he brought his arm around her. She laced her fingers through his hair at the back of his head. "There's a chance we don't succeed during this."

"There's always that chance, Coop." She took a calming breath and focused on the endgame—getting Fisher his daughter back and justice for the Fitzgeralds and Davidsons. "But we do our job and hope for the best."

"You've grown from an ambitious woman to someone even braver or stronger than I would've thought." He lifted his head and stared into her eyes. "I take that back. I've always known you'd be like this."

"Thank you," she said, letting herself enjoy the compliment. "Being a woman in this field, I can't afford to show weakness. I am strong, and I work hard, but the second I don't stay positive, I lose credit."

"So you're saying you're scared but won't admit it?"

"Scared? No. I know we can handle anything thrown at us. Worried about casualties? Yes. Always." She ripped up a little piece of napkin and contemplated their next move. "We should go to the hospital, then stop by the place she worked."

He moaned in protest. "I'm fine."

"No. It looks bad if we don't follow what we would normally do. We need to look normal."

"It could take hours. We don't have hours, Ads."

"Oh honey, haven't you learned? We're paranormals. We can speed up the process."

"I cannot believe you charmed your way to the front of the line. You rascal," Cooper said as they exited the ER an hour later. He was concussed and needed to rest—which they both knew he wouldn't do—but the routine worked. She saw two men from the precinct at the hospital, which confirmed her suspicion. They didn't wear uniforms, but it was clear they were being watched.

"You're not going to like my plan."

"Great, can't wait to hear it."

"It requires going back to the hotel room."

"I'll get behind that, hell yeah." He put his arm around her and pulled her against him, crushing his lips against hers and releasing a deep sigh. She put a hand to his chest to push him away, but her body betrayed her.

He kissed with passion and an unmatched energy. He nipped her upper lip and teased her with his tongue before retreating. His answering smile gave her butterflies, and she traced her wet lips with her fingers. "Uh, what was that for?"

"To continue our cover since dumb and dumber are hanging out by the gift shops like fucking creepers."

"Ah, makes sense."

"That was the official answer. My real motivation was because you're so goddamn cute fretting over me." He kissed her forehead and ran his hands up and down her arms. "I like it...you bossing me around and making sure I'm fine."

"You make it sound dirty."

"I mean, if you wanted to strip down and boss me around in bed, I wouldn't oppose."

She snorted, and they walked out the double doors and to the SUV. They were being tracked, but there was no recollection of having the car weaponized. She drove, since Cooper could barely keep his eyes open, and she waited until they were on the road before she broached the subject. "I'm going to need to investigate the restaurant myself."

"The fuck you are."

"You're concussed. You can't mess around with that. You need to rest for later."

"You are not going alone," he spit out, growling as she shook her head. "Addyson, no. This is dangerous."

"I interview drug pins and battle all sorts of assholes every day. This is no different."

"You can take care of yourself, I'm sure. But this goes deep. I won't risk it."

"Not your choice now, is it? I've been surviving just fine on my own for years, bud. Years."

"Nice math." He grunted and winced when he looked up into the sun. She laughed and hummed with a smug *told you so.* "Shut up, Ads. Fine. I hate this plan, by the way."

"Noted."

She drove to the hotel and dropped off a very disgruntled and pissed off Cooper before backing out and entering the restaurant's address into her phone. It was only a ten-minute drive, but she overthought everything in that short time.

She'd promised herself she'd never forgive him for how he'd left. She'd replayed in her head the things she'd say if she saw him again, and yet, she'd said *nothing* to that sort. After spending years together, she'd come home to a note that said *I can't do this anymore. I'm out, Ads. I'm sorry.*

His number had gone out of service. He'd dropped off all social media. He'd disappeared. At first, she'd thought something had happened to him. But time went on, and eventually, she'd stopped reaching out to him. He'd left her, with a goddamn note and no way to contact him. Worry had eaten at her, but that shifted to pain and anger. It had taken months before the feelings shifted to sadness, but the leftover fury had remained. He'd told her his reasons, and she had to either accept them or don't.

She let him kiss her, kissed him back, and her heart ached. Forgiveness wasn't easily given, but she knew she couldn't string him along if she didn't intend to try again. He acted different, regretful even. It reminded her how easy and wonderful it used to be with him, but what if he left again? If she put her heart on the line a second time, and he hurt her, she'd be a damn idiot.

She hit the wheel and chewed on a hangnail, hating the turmoil and uncertainty at his sudden appearance in her life. What the hell was she doing with Cooper? Were they going to run off into the sunset? He lived in California, and she lived in Phoenix. She wouldn't give up her career for him, and sure, maybe he'd move to Phoenix, but would the guy who left a Post-it note uproot his career? Would her branch of SSS even want him?

Focus.

She could put her all into the job, which was one of the main reasons she kicked ass at it. If she didn't tread carefully, Cooper could become a distraction—a terrible distraction who kissed her with an intensity she hadn't be able to find since he left. And she'd tried.

Her phone signaled to turn right, and she did, noticing a Ford Taurus following her in her rearview mirror. They were subtle, keeping a few cars' distance between them. She changed lanes and waited. They did too. She turned left at the gas station and sped down an alley, waiting for a beat to see if they followed. A few seconds went by, and she exhaled, almost ready to relax, when the damn car came into view. *Shit.* A prickle of fear went through her body when she tried reading the driver's memories, but nada. They blocked her. *The Chief.*

She dialed Cooper's number, relieved that he'd demanded she take his in case something happened. It rang four times without answer, and the prickle turned to a full flow. Why wasn't he answering? Did something happen to him? Did he pass out?

Could he defend himself if someone tried to attack him?

Her heartrate spiked. She thought about returning to the hotel, but he called back, and the instant relief frightened her. "Cooper," she said, unable to hide her distress.

"Where are you?" he barked, his voice stronger than when she'd left. "Are you okay?"

"I'm fine." She took a calming breath. "I'm being followed—it's Nate. I can't get a read on him."

"Does he know he's been spotted?"

"Probably." She continued back onto the main road and wiped her sweaty palms on her thighs. "I went into an alley to see if I imagined it, and he followed."

"Get on the main road."

"Already am."

"Good girl." Something rustled in the background. "I'll head there."

"No, you need to rest. If I don't call you in twenty minutes, find him." She swerved right, pulled into the parking lot, and made sure her knife rested at her ankle and her gun remained holstered on her hip. Defending herself wasn't an issue, but being blindsided was always a fear. "Twenty minutes, starting now."

"Be safe, Ads. Please."

"Always am."

She hung up, put on Chapstick, messed with the radio, and waited to see what the Taurus would do. Would he get out and attack? Would he crash into her? Cause a scene?

It drove by, but instead of going further down the road, it turned into an alley and went out of sight. *Thank God.* She could handle him but didn't want to. Not yet. Not when she needed to find Fisher's daughter.

She inhaled slowly, took note of her surroundings, and stepped out of the car. A few scattered trucks lined the parking lot, and a soft thud of music carried over from the outside speakers. The white brick walls were worn and weathered. If she drove by, she'd think it a hole-in-the-wall burger place. A local favorite. It did not have the appearance of a restaurant that would have a lot of patrons—but she knew it was more about the back area than the food.

She pushed the door open, and the smell of grease assaulted her nose. Her eyes stung from the stench, and she winced. The seated area was only a few feet from the kitchen and grill area. She bet every one of them reeked like fried food when they left the place.

She searched each person's mind quickly, scanning their thoughts and looking for memories of the Chief. Only, nothing happened. No recollections. Empty slate. She narrowed her eyes and pushed harder at the employees visible. The cook, waiters, hostess... She couldn't read them, and when a tall man with arms three times the size of hers looked up, she shivered from the cold, dead look in his eyes.

His mind rivaled a vault and he shut it down. Her skin hummed, yet no satisfaction rang from reading his thoughts. His jaw tensed, and she felt every stare pointed her direction. *Think fast.*

"Hi, I'm here to talk to your boss about Kayla's disappearance," she said, using her charisma to try and charm the terrifying man. She needed to save the situation before it worsened. Her skin prickled with unease and sweat dripped down her spine. Her charm didn't work. His scowl deepened, and the vile look in his eyes shook her core. He lifted one large arm and grunted as he pointed toward a black door. She'd seen this exact one in Fisher's memories. It was the only form of invitation she'd get, so she nodded at him before walking past him. Her weapon rested against her in its case, she was strong—could handle anything—and when she pushed the door open, she did not expect the blow to the head.

She had two seconds for a thought before everything went black.

Cooper.

8

SHE WASN'T ANSWERING HER PHONE, AND FIFTEEN MINUTES HAD passed. Cooper had trusted his gut most of his life, and it had never steered him wrong before. Something wasn't right, and he would be damned if he ignored it. His head pounded like a motherfucker, but he swallowed some pills, reholstered his weapon, and hurried the hell out of the hotel room. If anything happened to Addyson, he wasn't sure what he would do.

Go on a killing revenge spree?

Hurt every single living thing that hadn't protected her?

God, he couldn't think like that. It made his head and heart hurt more than he could handle. He just found her again. A future without her wasn't one he could even imagine, and he focused on the facts.

She was tough.

She'd already saved his ass once that day.

She was good at her job.

He repeated the mantra as he waited for a cab driver to arrive. It took ten minutes, but each second passing was like a knife to the gut. Worrying was easier to do when he lived hundreds of miles away and didn't know the details of her work.

And with the Police Chief running the show, it wasn't a good sign.

A yellow cab pulled into the drive of the hotel, and he jumped into the backseat. "Al's Diner, as fast as you fucking can, man."

"Good evening to you, too, sir," the driver said, going wide-eyed like she had never heard a cuss word before. "H-having a good day?"

"No. Someone I know could be in trouble." His voice was way too clipped and rude, but he didn't care. "So step on it."

"Will do, sir." The engine roared as she veered back onto the main road, and her grip tightened on the wheel. "You have business with Al?"

"Potentially. Tell me about him."

"Ah, I don't know him personally. Parents never let me go to that place. Over the years, rumors have grown about him having a mob connection, and my mom lost her sister to the mob back east, so we're wary." She took a sip of water and continued. He noted how her hand trembled when she brought the bottle to her mouth. "Can't say I've never driven over there at night, though. They close later than the bars, so if I ever need quick cash..."

"You hang out."

"Yes," she answered with a shaky voice. "Interesting crowd goes there."

"You ever drive Kayla home? Or any of the Davidson family?"

She paled and nodded. His already thin patience evaporated. With Addyson still not fucking answering his call, he needed to use all tools at his disposal. He pushed thoughts onto the young girl to tell him what he wanted to know.

"She called for a cab one night, and I went, waited for fifteen minutes, and when she came out, it looked like she tried to bolt. She sprinted from the back door and into the alley where I was, but someone stopped her, and I panicked. The guy yelled at her, and he held a gun, and..."

"And what?"

"I left, okay? I left. She could've needed help, and I left. I hate myself for it."

"Did you report it?"

"No."

"Do you know when it was? The date? And would you recognize the man if you saw a picture?"

"Probably. It was dark, but he was big. Bulky, even."

"Pull over a couple blocks away from the place, alright? We don't need to be seen." He found a photo of the Chief and waited until she did as he asked. They were still on the main road, but it wouldn't look as noticeable when he arrived on foot. Plus, he liked studying his surroundings before entering without backup. "Now, when did this happen?"

The girl blinked and took a nervous breath. "The Friday she went missing."

"Where did she have you taking her? Did she give an address?"

"Airport, which I thought was weird because it was the middle of the night. Oh, my god. Do you think she tried running away?"

"No one can say." He bordered on the side of annoyance. She could've reported this and helped the case, but he also knew if she'd put herself on the Chief's radar, something could've happened to her or her family. "Do you recognize this man?"

She stared and blinked fast before nodding. "That was him. Why is he dressed in... Oh, damn it. He's a cop. I'm fucked."

"Listen to me. Who else knows about this night? Anyone else? Your family?"

"No. No one. I don't know why I even told you," she said, crying.

"Keep it that way." He tossed her a twenty. "Go home and don't answer the door for anyone. Make sure your family stays there until tomorrow."

"What's tomorrow?"

"My deadline to nail this bastard." He gritted his teeth and stared at the diner. "I don't fail at what I do."

"But what if—"

"Nope. No what ifs. It's a rule. Now, what are you going to do? Repeat it back to me."

She wiped her eyes with her hands, leaving a trail of black around her cheeks, and repeated his instructions to a tee. "Thank you for not making me feel bad."

"Hey, there's a chance if you said anything about that night, he'd come after you. So go."

"Thank you. What's your name?"

"Don't worry about it." He smiled, exited the cab, and waited for her to turn off the street before marching toward the diner. Adrenaline was a magnificent thing, and it helped battle the headache that seemed to get duller by the second. One name kept replaying in his mind.

Addy.

He shouldn't have let her go alone, even though he couldn't have stopped her. He tried calling her again, but he knew she wouldn't answer. It wasn't like her to play games, and that meant something had happened. He watched the doors for a minute, trying to place where the cameras were, and he about shit himself when Fisher ran out of the place looking all sorts of flustered. Cooper sprang into action and caught up to the retreating man in no time. He yanked on the back of his collar, and the weasel yelped like a chihuahua.

"What!" he screamed, his eyes going wide when his attention focused on Cooper. "Oh shit. Shit."

"Start talking, now." He commanded him to speak the truth, and his veins hummed as the traitor started blabbing.

"He monitored me. He knew I met with you two, and...and... I told him our plan because he'd be able to tell if I lied to him and your partner is in there and he's going to use her to get what he wants and—"

"Shut the fuck up. Is Addy okay?" He tightened his grip on Fisher's neck and saw the fear in the man's eyes. Fear motivated people. "Your life doesn't matter to me. Your daughter's and Addy's do. Yours does not. Keep that in mind."

Fisher cried and snot ran down his nose when he bobbed his head up and down. "She's alive. She's breathing. He tied her up. Trying to find out how much she knows."

"She won't crack," he said with all the confidence in the world. "Not her."

Fisher shivered, and a dark, troubling look crossed his face. "He has ways of getting what he wants, Braxton."

Cooper's blood chilled. He tossed Fisher onto the ground and barged through the doors of the building without a second thought. He broke protocol but didn't give a shit. He'd handle paperwork later. Addy's life weighed more than that. A waitress screamed and dropped a plate of food. A hostess gasped and jumped back at the sight of him. He didn't stop. "Where's Nate?"

A panicked chef pointed toward a swinging door without a window, and he went through. The smell of smoke greeted him. He waved the puff away and squinted, letting his eyes adjust to the darkness around him. His muscles tensed, and the music boomed through the walls. With his hand near his gun, Cooper took in the surroundings. His attention landed on the guy in question. The Chief sat on a burgundy couch, smoking a cigar, holding a glass of amber liquid, and wearing an evil smile. Cooper wanted to bash his face in.

"Where is she?" he demanded.

"Ah, your friend? Hm. I can't recall what we did with her." Nate laughed and took a large swig of the amber liquid. "She is a looker, isn't she? I see why Fisher would've taken a chance at her, even though he is a dickless man."

"Answer the question." He moved closer to the Chief and didn't care that some dancers and patrons stared in their direction. He didn't care a fucking bit. "It takes one call for me to ruin you."

"Sure, but what will happen to Kayla and Fisher's annoying daughter? You won't risk their lives."

"I'm not Addyson. My moral compass broke a few years back, so if you want to try me, go ahead." He glared at the beast of a man, thinking of a million ways to get information out of him, none of them pleasant. "You have five seconds before I make the call."

The Chief's gaze shifted an inch to the left, and Cooper took off in that direction, inserting thoughts into every human in the room to alert him if Nate pulled a gun. He took three steps down the hall before someone shouted. He ducked as a bullet flew over his head and landed in the bright red wall.

Asshole had tried to kill him.

Doors lined the hallway on each side, and if he'd had time to digest what happened in each room, he'd punch walls. Rescuing Addy out of this place remained top priority. He opened the first door, and an older man and a naked woman greeted him. He slammed the door shut. The third and fourth doors were no different. Naked men, young women. He tried the last one, but the lock wouldn't budge. He shoved it with zero luck. *Damn.* He pulled out his gun and shot the handle. Bullets grazed the wall just inches from his head. The fucker almost shot him *again.*

His temper flared, and adrenaline coursed through him, his need to survive and find Addy guiding him. He stopped short the second he entered the room. The air left his lungs, and he fisted his hands. Disgust and relief combined into a sick sensation that caused him to release a pent-up breath. *She's alive.*

A little girl wore a filthy dress and held a teddy bear to her chest. Large headphones covered her ears, and her eyes widened with fear. He shut the door behind him.

He approached her slowly, smiling as he removed the headphones from her.

"Hey, sweetie, you okay?" he asked in the softest voice he could. "Is Fisher your dad?"

She nodded, looking so terrified she squeaked, and his heart plummeted. What kind of horrors had she witnessed? He shook the thought out of his mind. Getting her out of here trumped any sort of revenge he wanted on Nate.

"I'm here to save you. Your dad misses you so much. He's been worried. Have you seen him today?"

She shook her head and blinked back tears. The poor girl would be traumatized. The place stunk, was dark as hell, and the walls shook from music. She'd need therapy and a lot of hugs from her dad. He pressed one button to ring Patricio.

"Go for Pat."

"Send everything you got to my location. Addyson is missing, a child is being held hostage, and I bet I find the Davidsons here —if they're alive. Fast as you fucking can, Patricio."

"Consider it done."

A tiny sliver of relief started the spark of hope. They might get out of here intact. He needed time, though.

The hope shattered when the sound of bullets hit the outside of the metal door. He picked up the girl and put her on his back —they needed to escape this shithole. He willed anyone he could to stop what they were doing and throw anything they could into the hallway. The place couldn't be filled with only paranormals.

His veins hummed like an electric current blasted through him, but he kept going. He'd only overused his ability once before, but he would do whatever he could to get the girls—Fisher's daughter and Addy—out of there safely.

Show me where she is. He commanded those he could to listen.

It challenged him to focus on three things simultaneously, but being a paranormal had its perks. The sounds of furniture sliding and doors opening meant his plan to slow Nate down had worked. With a quick glance down the hall, he saw commotion.

Shouts and furniture and arguing. The people in the rooms stood in the hallway, some naked, others not.

He took off running in the opposite direction of the noise and glanced into each opened room, feeling bile rise up at the scenes meeting him. He would make Nate pay for this place. This shit wasn't legal and the fucker needed to go.

The girl's grip around his neck tightened, and he winced when she cut off his airway. She smelled like vomit and sweat, and he reached up to give her a reassuring pat on the arm. "I'll get you out of here. I promise."

She whimpered in response.

Everything slowed when he arrived at the end of the hall—there was no door, no windows to escape through—and a second wave of worry hit him. Nate stood a few yards away, holding a gun with innocents around him.

I need a plan. Right fucking now.

9

Her head hurt like a bitch, and her wrists stung as she tugged on the restraints. She let herself freak out for one second. He could've killed her instantly and he didn't.

That was his mistake. Cooper would find her. She knew it deep within her bones and would bet her life on it. It wasn't a matter of if, rather a matter of when, and she had to survive until then. The zip ties were too tight, and she searched her mind for a tutorial she'd watched years ago on how to escape them. It required moving her hands around so her wrists touched and the lock was directly in the center. Her skin glistened with sweat, so it made it a bit easier to wiggle the restraint around to get to the prime hand position, and she slammed them down.

"Shit." It didn't work.

She adjusted the lock to make it more center and tried again. *Bingo.* She released a breath of relief as she tossed the pieces to the ground. If Nate tried to manhandle her again, she would break his neck. She rubbed her temples to help ease the pain from being clocked on the head, but it didn't do any good.

Sounds of gunfire made her bolt up, amped and ready to go. She tried slamming into the door, hoping the lock would budge, but no luck. Searching her pockets for anything sharp and groaned in frustration. She smelled like sweat and her heart raced. The *pop pop pop* outside her door made her adrenaline soar. She chewed her lip and eyed the small, enclosed room. Old wallpaper with edges rolling up from dampness surrounded her. Ceiling tiles with leak stains and rust rested above. A used, gross bed sat in one corner. A small chair stood off to the side, and she shivered at the thought of all the things that had been done in this room.

The side table. Addy jumped into action and lifted the chair and placed the four legs on top of the small table. It'd give her just enough height to reach the ceiling. She carefully hoisted herself onto the chair and waited, hoping the table and legs didn't break.

The ceiling tiles moved easily, and the noises in the hall grew louder. Wooden planks crisscrossed above the tiles created a few beams that she could walk on.. Thundering footsteps and Nate barking angry orders meant one thing: Cooper had arrived. She closed her eyes and felt the zing in her body when she read the memories of those around her. She'd learned her radius neared ten feet. She could sense through barriers, but if anyone stood behind the ten feet perimeter, she'd get nothing.

Visions of Cooper dodging bullets, picking up a little girl, and running down the hall flooded her mind.

A fierce relief went through her. *He's here. He's okay. The little girl will survive.* But she'd also seen Nate, furious and shooting at random. That wouldn't do.

Addyson hoisted herself up, pausing as the weight beneath her shifted. She needed to swing onto the wooden beam a few feet away. Her muscles burned as she lifted herself up, hoisted a leg around, and pushed into sitting position. The hallway was to the left—so she carefully crawled along the beam that direction. The tiles were loosely placed, and one ounce of pressure too much would send her flying to the ground, but the wood supported her. Her heart beat in her throat, and the fear would've paralyzed most people. But not her. She focused on the task and made a plan. One careful movement at a time.

It smelled like mildew and plaster, and she breathed in through her nose, out through her mouth as she picked up her knee and set it down a couple inches further. The wood held and she repeated the process. It felt like an hour had passed by the time she made any progress, and she lifted a corner of one tile to survey the scene below.

If she scared easily, the scene would've made her gasp. Nate pointed his gun at Cooper, who held the little girl behind him, shielding her. She needed to distract Nate, stop him, do anything to cause him to pause. If he shot Cooper, he'd do significant damage to both him and the girl.

God, her mind raced. What would make Nate forget about Cooper? What would make him hesitate?

Get him talking.

Buy time.

Use myself as a shield for the child.

Her gut told her to mention Kayla. All those memories of her and Nate stood fresh in Addy's mind. Kayla meant something to him.

She searched for Fisher, hoping to find a memory containing anything he might've hidden about Kayla, but she came up empty. She did note a man who looked to be Nate's sidekick, and she felt the familiar humming of her powers working. He knew where Kayla was.

Bingo.

Without a second to spare, she moved over the wooden beam and jumped down onto the Chief's back, disarming him with one smooth motion and landing so his face smashed against the ground. She kicked the gun toward Cooper and called Patricio.

"Get off me, you piece of shit!" Nate yelled, but she dug her knee into his neck. He sounded nothing like the manipulative asshole he was. He screamed and thrashed as he tried throwing Addyson off him but failed.

"Patricio, check the safehouse. Two cross streets are Heatherton and Willowcrest. Kayla is there, and I'm guessing the rest of her family is, too," Addy said, watching the color leave Nate's face.

"I'll send a unit now. We're on our way. Nice work, Addy." He hung up, and while the threat lessened with Nate restrained, she wouldn't relax until Nate wore cuffs, Fisher reunited with his daughter, and Kayla and her family were safe.

"Why her? What did she do?" she asked Nate while motioning for Cooper to walk past them with the girl. He gave her a reassuring nod, but she saw the relief in his eyes. She felt it, too.

Nate squirmed underneath her, and she applied more pressure than necessary. "Answer me."

He growled and tried spitting at her. She shoved his face a little harder to the ground. "Have it your way. I'll make sure we document every single thing that happened here. Starting with girls who are sixteen, underage drinking, the—"

"Fuck! Kayla witnessed something she shouldn't have."

"So you took her entire family and killed another?"

"She could've told them. I protected what's mine. That little bitch wasn't going to get me in trouble."

"Wrong you are." She laughed and kept a smile on her face when the sounds of sirens greeted her in the background. "Unlike you, I take pride in holding those accountable when they abuse their power. Kayla deserved better. The Fitzgeralds deserved better."

"I had nothing to do with them. Not a damn thing. You'll see."

The doors burst open, and Patricio entered with a slew of his guys surrounding him. Addyson greeted him with a smile. "He's all yours, Pat."

"Fisher in here? Cooper mentioned he double-crossed you."

Addy frowned as the thought about his daughter caused her chest to tighten. "If he is, I haven't seen him. He's a mess...manipulated to the point I don't think he could function."

"We need to apprehend him. Go find Cooper. We'll check in later."

She nodded and left Nate to her boss, then jogged down the hall and out into the main area, scanning the crowd of people for the one pair of broad shoulders she wanted to see. He stood there, laughing, one hand held by the little girl. A sudden thought hit her. She could see the two of them with a daughter. She would have his coloring and her hair, his smile, and—

Oh my god. What am I doing?

He'd been back in her life for a day—and they weren't *together*. They weren't anything more than colleagues who'd hooked up. She shouldn't be thinking about that shit. Not now. When his gaze landed on hers, he stopped talking to those by him and stalked toward her, Fisher's daughter in tow. He didn't ask permission before crushing her against his chest, wrapping his arm around her, and hugging her like their first time together. "Addy," he said, the warmth in his voice sending silly thoughts through her mind.

She took in his masculine scent and admitted to herself she wasn't ready to let him go. "You're okay? She's okay?"

"Fuck that guy. But yes, she's fine. We're buds now." He pulled back and looked down at her, a smile playing on his lips, then cupped Addy's chin. "I need to kiss you. Seeing you come out of the ceiling terrified me even though it was extremely hot."

"Yeah?" she teased and closed the distance between their mouths. He met her kiss with an unbridled passion, making them both groan. Agents surrounded the place, and they were still on the job. She giggled against his lips, and he slid his hands down her sides until they landed on her hips.

"You all good? All in one piece?" he asked while assessing her. "When you didn't answer your phone..." He shivered.

"Not here." She lightly traced the bruises around his eyes with her finger. "We got the girl, found the bad guy, and lived to tell the tale. Job well done, Braxton."

"Job fucking well done, Ads. We make a good team."

Someone walked in the door, signaling the little dig of the bell, and when Fisher appeared, Cooper's entire body stiffened. He moved, fingers already clenched into a fist, and Addy followed him. She knew that face and stance. Fisher stood no chance.

"You dumb fucker," Cooper said, drawing the attention of everyone there.

"Look! He-e-e was going to h-hurt her!" He held up his hands and cried, and Addy reached over and squeezed Cooper's arm. He stilled, looked at where her fingers rested on his wrist, and took a deep breath.

"Not worth it, Coop."

"The only reason I'm not beating his face in is because his daughter and you survived. There's no saying what would've happened if the outcome had differed."

She weaved her arm through his as Patricio returned from the hall with Hansen and a handcuffed Chief. Her boss looked like he'd won the lottery. Big eyes, large smile, jovial laugh. "Davidsons are alive. Our guys found the safehouse. They look rough, but they're breathing. Heading to the hospital once I lock his ass up."

"And the techs?" she asked, seeing a few of the IT team from the office in the diner. "Our original plan backfired."

"Doesn't matter. We'll retrieve all the info before one of his guys deletes all the evidence. I'm real glad they showed up early. Already found quite a few files of blackmail. He planned on using it to get vixens, vamps, even wolves, to do his dirty work." Patricio clapped a hand on her shoulder as he walked out. "We'll take your statements, but it will be an hour or so before we need you down there. Clean up your injuries, relax, then come in. Use the back door, though, it'll be a media nightmare."

"Got it, boss," she replied, snapping her fingers. "He took my gun. If you can find it, I'd like it back."

He nodded, and a high-pitched scream echoed through the chamber. Addy and Cooper jumped apart, tense and ready for action. She searched for the source, already planning her next steps, then spotted Fisher weeping loudly and without shame as he hugged his daughter. Cooper and she shared a look of under-standing. Parents knew no limits when it came to their child's safety, and despite Cooper being pissed at Fisher, she understood the guy's motivations. His daughter should always remain top priority, so she couldn't exactly fault him for his behavior. "I'll be right back."

She strolled outside and knocked on Patricio's car window before he left. He raised a brow at her, signaling her to speak. "Fisher acted under duress, psychological torture, and having his daughter held hostage. I will not be pressing any charges against him for a single thing. I want that known."

"I won't either," Cooper said, joining her at her side. His warmth seeped into her, and she wanted to lean against him.

"Noted." Patricio nodded at the pair before driving away. Chatter surrounded the couple, but Addyson tuned it out. Cooper spun her around and ran his large hands up and down her arms, clasping her fingers in his as he stared at her with the smirk she'd fallen in love with years ago.

"I need to check every inch of your body to make sure you're not hurt."

She blushed and found herself smiling despite the shitstorm going on. "Every inch, huh?"

"Every single one," he said, lowering his voice before pressing a kiss on the top of her head. "I've had a semi hard-on since you kicked the shit out of Nate. We might need to role play."

Cooper barely walked into the room before he picked her up, and she wrapped her legs around his waist. He pushed her against the door. "Fuck, Ads. I need you."

She arched her back and pulled his hair, bringing him even closer to her. The adrenaline rush from solving a case was inexplicable, and the release of endorphins combined with an orgasm... Her body shook with a desperate, needy plea. Cooper had survived, she'd survived, and they'd won today's battle. The combination of everything put her senses on high alert. Each brush of his fingers on her skin made her shiver. His breath tickled her ear and neck, and his sweaty scent had her wanting to lick each bead of moisture from his body. "Shirt off," she demanded.

Cooper reached behind his head and yanked the black shirt onto the floor. She groaned at the sight of his muscular chest. A soft dusting of hair coated his pecs, and she ran her fingers over the hard-earned muscle. She needed to taste it, but at the pace they were going, she didn't have time. Her pulse throbbed between her thighs, and she couldn't satiate the craving for him. She wanted everything, hard and fast, slow and long.

"You're looking at me with bedroom eyes, baby. It's my favorite expression on you ever." He unbuttoned her shirt while she admired his tense jawline. He tossed it to the ground and undid her bra in one quick motion. He cupped her heavy breasts, his fingers gently teasing her nipples. She shivered, head to toe, and moaned.

"Let's make sure you're okay here." He pressed a quick kiss on her neck and collarbone. "Here." Then her cleavage. "Here and here." He teased and nipped each breast and sucked a pert tip into his mouth, grazing his teeth over it.

"Christ," she purred at the warm sensation of his lips on her skin. Her knees buckled. He reached behind her to hold her up as he continued licking and teasing her breasts. Her entire body buzzed with desire and lust, and her thoughts went wild. She bucked against him, and it caused him to suck harder.

He dragged his tongue over her skin, groaning. "Can't get enough." He moved them to the bed, and they stripped off the rest of their clothes in a matched frenzy. Cooper tossed his pants and boxers to the side. When she removed her panties, he stared at her with so much emotion in his eyes her breath hitched in her throat.

"Addy," he said, crawling over her so an arm rested on each side of her face. "You feel it too."

She closed her eyes when he started kissing her slowly. She angled her hips against him and felt the head of his cock teasing her. He winced and pushed up to look down at her. "I don't have a condom."

"I'm on birth control, Coop." She wanted to feel him. All of him, every inch inside her and beneath her skin. "I'm safe."

"I can go down on you again." He spoke through clenched teeth, and she arched her back so his dick lined up with her center. "Fuck, are you sure?"

"Please, babe, I need to feel you," she admitted, loving how his entire face glowed with her words. That expression lit her up inside. He used to stare at her like that before, and to see it again after all this time made her heart soar.

He groaned as he thrust inside her with admirable control. She wanted him hard and fast, so she could feel him deep inside where he stretched her walls. But Cooper went slow and steady. In and out. He spread her thighs wide and gripped her ass with his hands as sweat pooled between their chests. He kissed her neck, burying his face in the crook of it. His entire body tensed as he ground into her.

The scent of his skin remained the same, and the two time-lines in her mind merged.

It was like three years before, but better. He'd grown bigger. Stronger. More focused. She was wiser, appreciated how giving he'd always been. His body had aged with grace, hers became more sensitive.

"You feel like home, Ads," he said between thrusts. "Fuck, I want this forever."

"Big words, Cooper." Her voice came out between pants. The pressure built around her core, and her muscles tensed. "I'm close, so close."

He responded by holding her tighter and fucking her harder. He held nothing back and slammed into her, whispering promises about the future as she came around him. Her legs shook, her vision blurred, and her chest heaved as she climaxed so hard it almost hurt. Cooper followed seconds later, and she swallowed his cries in her mouth.

He'd always come loudly, and the fact that hadn't changed made her laugh. Her giggles stilled when he rolled and pulled her with him so she lay on his chest with him still inside her. "I can't lose you again. Whatever it takes, I'll do. Name it. *Please.*"

Her face warmed, and she traced his bottom lip with her thumb. "I won't do distance."

"I'll move here. With you, next door, down the block. I don't care." He kissed her and threaded his fingers in her hair, softly running through it with a half smile. "I never stopped loving you —the young and bright-eyed woman from three years ago. But I want the chance to love *this* version of you. We are good together."

"We are," she said, unable to stop her grin. "I need to take it slow."

"Slow as in, I get part of your closet until I can find a place of my own?" He had the longest eyelashes, and she'd always thought them beautiful. Such a tough man and hard face, but those lashes teased at the man beneath. "You didn't say no, so..."

"Sure. But you will get your own place, Cooper." She laughed when he put a hand over his heart and acted offended.

"Of course. But when I transfer to your office, we'll be traveling and working together a lot, so I won't be home..." He trailed off and gave her a sheepish smirk. "But we will go at your pace."

"Damn straight, Braxton."

"I love your bossy side." He picked her up and set her next to him before stretching. He took his time getting up from the bed and she admired the hard lines of his back. "Come on, Ads. Get your ass dressed, and let's head to the station to see Nate behind bars. It'll be our own sick version of foreplay."

She snorted and couldn't think of a better way to end the day.

10

THREE WEEKS LATER...

Cooper woke up with legs tangled in his and hair in his face. It took him a second to remember he'd stayed over with Addyson. He rolled her closer to him and cradled her head in his arms, sighing with utter content. It seemed like no time had passed since he'd held her last, and yet, things had changed for the better. They were grown, confident in who they were, and dedicated to a job they both loved.

He wouldn't lose her this time around. He'd already sent in his request to his boss to transfer, and until she pushed him away, she'd become his home. His partner wasn't fazed after hearing him talk about Addy for years and planned to come out and visit soon. He pressed a light kiss on her forehead, and she snuggled up against him, letting out a tiny snore.

God, he loved her.

It wasn't too soon. He knew all he needed to know about her, but he didn't want to scare her. It would have to wait. He'd broken some of her trust when he left, and he needed to earn it back. And he would, one step at a time.

He knew the moment she woke up. The soft breath hitting his

arm stopped, and she stilled in his arms. Them being together, naked again, was new, and he gave her a few seconds. "Morning, Ads."

"Did I sleep stalk you?" she asked, her voice all throaty and drowsy. It was cute.

"Nope. I pulled you closer to me." He lifted her chin up and kissed her, morning breath and all. "I like waking up with you."

"It's nice." She hummed and stretched her arms over her head, giving him a perfect view of her naked chest. Her nipples pebbled, and he reached over to tease one during her yawn. Goose bumps broke out along her skin. "Hey, you." She swatted his hand away but wore a playful look on her face. "We have work today."

"I understand." He grabbed her hips and picked her up so she straddled him. Her hair landed just above her chest, and her smooth and warm skin teased him. Sleep lines covered her body from the sheets, and he couldn't get enough of her. Even after spending almost every night together the last three weeks, he only saw her. "You look so fucking good in the morning."

She bit her lower lip and wiggled against his cock. She laughed when he arched his hips so it pressed against her center. "Last night not enough for you?" she purred.

"Ads," he started but stopped when she reached down to position his dick to slide inside her. "*Fuck.*"

"You were saying?" she teased, rocking her body at a slow pace that sent tingles up and down his body. Her wetness coated him. She knew the perfect pace to ride him, and he groaned when she bent down to put her tits in his face.

"Dangerous woman," he mumbled before taking one sweet nipple into his mouth and sucking it hard. She reacted so fiercely when he used his teeth and nibbled on it. She bucked and dug her nails into his chest. It fueled him. Her sounds, her scent, her ability to let loose with him. He held on to her hips and guided her to go faster, take him deeper, and ride him harder.

"*Yes*," she moaned as sweat dripped down her chest onto his. He never wanted sex to end with her. Their souls fucking intertwined when their mouths came together. She brought her lips to his, and he sucked her bottom lip into his mouth, cupping the back of her neck and deepening the kiss to the point he swallowed her screams. She whimpered as she came, the desperate, needy sounds at the back of her throat turning him on beyond reason, and he couldn't stop the words from leaving his mouth.

"I fucking love you." He felt the familiar stirring at the base of his spine, and pleasure hit him like a truck, the orgasm stealing all thoughts from his mind and air from his lungs, and he held on to his woman, riding it out.

She fell onto his chest with a loud sigh, and he swore he felt her kiss right above his heart. It took a few seconds for him to catch his breath, and when he did, he lifted her face to meet his eyes. She never remained this quiet, and he worried his words had freaked her out. "Addy—"

"Did you mean it?"

"Yes."

A shy look came over her before she burst into a smile. "Jesus, I didn't... I love you too. I didn't know it would be this fast, but shit, it's true."

His matching grin hurt his face.

But they didn't get time to celebrate their new feelings. Her phone went off, and she bounced up to get it. "It's Owings."

She paced the room—butt ass naked—and nodded to herself. It endeared him how fierce and badass she was for everyone else, but for him, she softened. She sat on the edge of the bed. "Uh huh. Sure."

She straightened her spine and gave him a worried look.

"Wait—the Fitzgeralds weren't a part of Nate's scheme?" Addyson asked, her hand going to her chest to rub circles. She did that when her nerves took over. Cooper joined her on the edge of the bed and massaged her neck. It didn't matter how many orgasms she had, her muscles were always tight.

"Okay, you want me to tell Cooper?" She chewed on her lip and nodded again. "I will. See you in an hour."

"What's going on?"

"The Fitzgerald's killer is still out there, and guess who they assigned the case to?"

"Nate didn't do it?" he asked, a flittering feeling of regret passing through him. "He as much as admitted it."

"Patricio said no. Thinks paras are involved." She started pulling on her underwear and workpants. "We head out in an hour. You okay partnering up again?"

That made him smile. "Partners for life, Addyson. Now let's go find these assholes."

Thank you for reading! Did you enjoy? Please add your review because nothing helps an author more and encourages readers to take a chance on a book than a review.

And don't miss the next book of the *Southwest Supernatural Society series* from E.L. Adams coming soon!

Until then, read more Mystic Owl books with THUNDERSTRUCK by Wren Michaels. Turn the page for a sneak peek!

Also be sure to sign up for the City Owl Press newsletter to receive notice of all book releases!

SNEAK PEEK OF THUNDERSTRUCK
BY WREN MICHAELS

Reseda never gave much thought to biological functions. But when they're ripped away, sometimes the littlest things stick out, like a body-convulsing sneeze, the sting of a scraped knee, or the tenderness of someone's lips in a kiss. Reseda jotted down the words *shudder, pain, soft,* and *wet.* She no longer connected with them. In fact, she had an entire journal of thoughts from a lifetime ago, when the word *life* had a different meaning.

So many years had gone by since her *rising.* Things blurred. Some faded completely. Maybe time eroded some memories to make room for new ones, perhaps more urgent and lifesaving ones. Those she could remember she compartmentalized into two types—*the before time* and *the rising.* She tucked the latest ones under the before time, when she was still human. Alive. Those were the things she journaled, kept safe and out of her head where people could pry. The military liked to do that, full of shrinks and doctors poking and prodding. They called it debriefing, but it was more for their safety than hers.

Sure, someone could read her journal, too. But to them, it would be a series of meaningless words that made no sense. But to Reseda, it was a map, a trail of breadcrumbs to who she used to be.

Something toiled in her mind. She couldn't give it a name, or she'd forgotten what to call it. All she had was a scratch at the back of her head telling her she should be scared. But fear never surfaced. Nothing ever did. No sense of emotion at all. Most of the time, her body and mind were weightless, as if waiting for someone to tell her how to act, how to think, how to feel.

She lived for the days she got to hunt, when she could get off the covert military base and run the floor of the Pacific Rim National Forest. When she had a purpose, something to fill the void inside her.

"Reseda," a loud voice distracted her from her thoughts. It belonged to her fellow operative, Teagan. "What's going on with you lately? I called your name like five times." Teagan planted her hands on her curvy hips. "Something's off. Do we need to have you checked out?"

Reseda rose from the floor and made her way to the bathroom. Teagan's long dark hair brushed against her as they bumped shoulders. She imagined it feeling like fine silk. "I'm fine. Just thinking."

"So, can I borrow your pin-striped corset for the show tonight? The one with the double-dagger holder? I want to test it out with the twins." Teagan spun them with precision before dotting each silver-coated tip with a kiss.

"Yeah, sure." Reseda nodded and shoved her earlier thoughts deep into a compartment in her mind. What good did it do to think about those kinds of things anymore, anyway?

"About the mission tonight? It's a standard sweep." Teagan followed, covering their shared room in three steps. The bare walls and drab blankets made the place as lifeless as her soul.

Reseda stared at her reflection, trying to identify with the face that looked back at her. Some days, she did her job, came back to her room, and never gave it another thought. But some days, like today, something poked at her, forced her to take a step back and reflect on where she had come from. A young woman born of two scientists from Guatemala. Then born again—but no longer among the living, helping the government eradicate a preternatural threat to the human race.

Funny how they required an equally unnatural life form to do it. Would her kind then, too, be eradicated once the wolf threat had been taken care of?

Reseda clenched a fist and studied it like a newborn discovering their hand for the first time. Long had her nerves been dead, all sensation from pleasure to pain eliminated. Blood dribbled through her fingers, and she stared at it, waiting for something to happen. Something to go off in her head that this was wrong. She should feel something. She should cry out.

Nothing.

Reseda turned her attention back to Teagan. "I'm good to go."

Teagan quirked a perfectly sculpted brow that complimented her flawless, light-brown skin. "Who you showing off to? It's just me here, and I can do that, too. So, what the hell's up with you?"

"Nothing. What's with the inquisition?" Reseda tilted her head and stared at Teagan, the closest thing to a friend Reseda had.

They didn't talk like human friends did, all giggly and happy. They didn't share make-up tips or gossip about guys, other girls, or even go out. But they had a common bond, a frame of reference no one else could share. It linked them.

Reseda had never asked Teagan if she ever thought of the past or if she wished she could be human again. Teagan never gave her any inkling she did.

"You're just not usually all spacey and shit. You're always on top of your game. So, if there's something wrong with you, especially tonight when our asses will be on the line sweeping for wolves, I need to know."

Reseda appreciated Teagan's blunt attitude, and Reseda could give it back in return without having to deal with backlash. Sometimes it helped not to have not to have to deal with the emotional bullshit of what ifs, hurt feelings, and misunderstandings. Just say what you mean and mean what you say.

That was the good part of the rising. Reaching that next level of consciousness, of doing what had to be done to save lives. They had each other's backs at all times, no question in loyalty or back-stabbing. They had a job to do and got it done.

They were all the same—The Dolls. Weapons made of flesh and blood, minus all the shit that got in the way. No pain to take them down in an attack. No emotions to question orders. No feelings to get in the way of decisions. Most of all, they were already dead, so they couldn't die again. At least not in any human way. They were as close to immortal as the government could get.

Teagan walked to Reseda's bed and picked up the journal. "You know, if Drake ever finds this, he'll hand you your ass."

Reseda ripped the book from Teagan's hands. "I don't give a shit what Drake thinks. So what if I write down some words I think about. What would make him flip out over that?"

"Mainly because my brother's an asshole," Teagan said, folding her arms. "Who just happens to be your commanding officer."

"He doesn't own me. We're not even technically military. We don't exist." Reseda air quoted the words. "We're the red-headed step-child the Canadian military refuses to acknowledge. Yet we're the ones saving everyone's asses." The government didn't want the public knowing about the threat that lived among them, that the monsters of lore were real. "Plus, Drake would have to take me down. And since no human possibly can..." Reseda stuffed the journal under her pillow.

"I know. But it would be fun to see him try and have you wail on him." Teagan tossed her head back in a laugh, her shiny curls bouncing with each chuckle.

"Well, if he ever does, I'm walking. I'm only here to help with the wolf problem. Not to be one of his little pretend tin-soldiers. Those wolves killed my dad. Now Drake said they're targeting my mom. There hasn't been a sighting of her in weeks. She could be out there fighting for her life somewhere. Once I wipe out this wolf infestation, I'm out of here anyway." Reseda changed into a tight black tank top and jeans, prepping for the mission.

"How's that gonna work, Reseda? You're not human. We have a hard enough time trying to keep the wolves and shit away from people. What happens when *you* start going out among them?" Teagan let out another laugh. "Like, what are you gonna do, work at a diner? You don't function like them, can't even interact with them anymore. You'll just come off as a bitch. You'd get fired on your first day."

"Whatever." Reseda flipped her the bird.

"Exactly." Teagan flopped onto the bed. "This is who we are now. This is our life. There's always going to be some kind of threat. Once we kick the wolves' asses, who's to say some other creature won't show up."

"I know there's other demons out there. But so far, none of them seem to be as ruthless and dangerous as the wolves." Reseda relied on those demons for information, and if Drake ever found out, he'd kill her sources. He wanted nothing to do with anything that wasn't human. Not that Reseda was a fan of them herself. But she was pretty sure he didn't even like The Dolls. The fact that Teagan was his sister was probably the only saving grace. Even then, Reseda wouldn't put it past him to turn on her.

At least The Dolls had a reason for their abrupt nature and dulled emotions. Drake was just a dick.

Reseda didn't know what the future held. She only knew it wouldn't involve being a government pawn the rest of her life. She'd already been a science experiment, a magical or mythical accident—take your pick. But some day, she'd have a life of her own again. She wouldn't belong to anyone or anything. Someday, she'd be free.

Free to do what? She didn't care, as long as she was in charge of her life, her destiny. That was all that mattered. For now, she'd play by other's rules until she got what she needed—answers.

"Let's go. I need a run and to crush some wolf skulls." Reseda snapped on her bracers and stared at Teagan.

Teagan nodded. "That's my girl."

Reseda used to relish the sting of the chilly autumn night on her cheeks as she ran, her heart pounding a relentless rhythm against her ribs. But labored breathing would have slowed her down as aching lungs struggled to take their fill of much-needed breath. She would have had to stop. She would have gotten killed.

Her long legs erupted into a full gallop as she raced through the woods, carefully weaving through the enormous redwood trees that dotted the edge of the Pacific Rim Forest. Darkness shielded her to all, except those she ran from. And she counted on it.

She glanced over her shoulder, eyeing the two shadows charging her at full speed, darting in and out between streaks of moonlight. A wry grin curved her lips as she turned back to face her target. She launched her body toward the branch and pulled herself up. Crouching, she waited for her predators—who would soon be her prey.

The two wolves halted beneath the tree, scrutinizing the area for any sign of her. As they tracked her scent, their heads turned, their attention drawn upward. She dropped from the tree and brought them down with her, a prompt heel to the face for one, the brunt of her closed fist for the other. Sharpened silver spikes shot from each of the bracers attached to her wrists and plunged into the chest cavities of her victims, piercing the hearts.

Howls rode the crisp breeze, releasing the dying souls. Once warm bodies turned cold as fur faded to graying flesh.

Seconds later, they exploded to dust.

What had become of Vancouver Island in the few short years since she'd been there? The bigger—and more disturbing—question was what would it turn into if she failed? Not only was her mother's life at stake, but all of mankind. She'd already lost her dad to the vile creatures who killed without remorse. But these days, so did Reseda.

For a brief moment, she wondered if she would have been able to kill a wolf when she was human. Perhaps not physically, but would she have had the mental capacity to take a life? Pitted against her own, probably. For the sake of others, though, could she have put her own life at risk? She liked to think so, that she would have still made a difference somehow in the world, ridding the evil that plagued it.

A twig snapped from behind her, startling her out of her thoughts. She pressed her body to the tree, grinding her back against the bark, waiting for the intruder to present itself. Stark green eyes peeked out under a mess of blond hair as a head popped up from the other side of the wide tree base.

"Marshall!" Reseda snapped. "¡Ay Dios mio!"

No wonder why the wolves were the superior species. Humans were always throwing themselves into harm's way. Marshall was probably the most vulnerable of them all. Sure, he could make a bomb from a yogurt cup and a piece of string, but in a fight, he'd end up lunch for the wolves.

Reseda thought back to when she'd been one of them, the ignorant. The naive. The living. Though she appeared human enough, acted it—for the most part, minus those pesky feelings and shit—she walked a fine line between living and dead. And without her, humans would end up on the endangered species list.

"Sorry." He raised his hands, taking a step back. "I knew you were out here, so I wanted to check in on you."

"Your ass needs to be in the lab, not out here in the field. What the hell were you thinking?" she demanded in a whisper. Marshall was the behind-the-scenes guy, the brains. Not a field agent, and certainly not able to go up against a wolf. She didn't understand his lack of common sense. It confused her. Why would he put himself in harm's way so needlessly?

"I had to see how the new bracers worked in action." He cocked his head. "This is scientific research. It's not like I was out for a jog at one in the morning for the hell of it."

"You're also a human. In a forest full of werewolves on a full moon. And *you're* supposed to be the genius?" She inched closer to him, narrowing her eyes. "I can't do my job if I have to protect you out here."

"I'm far from helpless against a couple of fur-bags, Reseda." He shoved his hands to his hips. "I do have a trick or two for my own protection. I make all your toys. As if I wouldn't make some for myself?"

It amazed her how Marshall came up with all those nifty inventions and weapons. Yet the thought of him actually using them in action seemed like the most ridiculous idea ever. She forced down a laugh as she pictured the tall, lanky dude clanking his way through the forest scaring only himself. The wolves would laugh, too, as they licked his blood from their fangs.

"Go. Now." She jerked her finger toward the hill. "If you don't, I'll march you back myself. I have a couple more rounds to do, then I'll check back in."

If she allowed Marshall to get himself killed, not only would her ass be on the line, but the rest of her team's, too. Marshall would say it was because they were friends. She'd say she was only protecting an investment.

All she had left in her life were investments. Investments in her time, in her team, and in a wolf-free future for the humans. Relationships and friendships came with something she couldn't give back—feelings.

"Where are the rest of The Dolls?"

"On patrol. Where I need to be," Reseda said. At least they should be. Neither Teagan nor Dahlia, another one of the operatives, had checked in with her in hours. But both were well trained assassins like Reseda and could handle themselves.

Marshall stared at her. His lingering gaze perplexed her, as if he were trying to dig for something behind her eyes. Then his expression softened. "Yeah, I'm worried, too."

"I don't do *worry*, Marshall," Reseda said. "It's not in my genetic makeup anymore."

He sighed. "It is more than you think."

Reseda cocked a brow as she studied him, repeating the words in her head. What did he mean by that?

"Would you two crank it up a notch, 'cuz I don't think the dogs down the hill heard you," a gruff voice said from behind them.

"Great, Captain Constant-Wedgie is here. Now the party can begin," Marshall groaned.

"Don't give him a higher rank than he deserves." Reseda rolled her eyes at Marshall before turning to the soldier. "Drake, what the hell? Why is everyone in my zone tonight?"

Reseda had shit to do, and all these interruptions meant more lives in danger. The menfolk needed to release their testosterone and always pulled her into the middle of it. She really didn't understand men sometimes. The more she was around them, the less she really wanted to.

"I wasn't until I heard you two arguing. The lab rat needs to be back in his cage, and you need to be hunting." Drake eyed the length of her.

Sarcasm was his only defense, and he sucked at it. He was lucky he was a pretty boy and his bourbon-colored biceps looked good holding a gun.

"I'm working on it. You're not helping the situation. Go check on the girls. I'll handle Marshall," she said.

"You're out of order, Ms. Juarez." Drake's haughty tone reflected the harshness of his eyes. "You need to get back on the hunt."

"*¡Puchica!* You can kiss my ass, Drake." She wanted to do a lot more than just tell him off. But she had to remember to play nice with the government in order to keep receiving any available intel on locating her mother. Even if that meant dealing with Drake. But she didn't have to like him, and she made that fact clear from the start.

Her fingers clenched into a fist, itching to punch the guy. Or maybe strangle him. Something scratched at her brain at the very sight of the man. If she only knew what.

Drake's nostrils flared as his glare intensified. "*Araneae.*"

A groan burst from her lips as she dropped to her knees, wrapping her arms around herself.

Tiny legs pricked at her skin as spiders crept up her body. They crawled everywhere—her hair, arms, legs, inundating every part of her. Venomous fangs dug into her eyes, nose, and lips. Blood stained her nails as she clawed at her skin to get them off. A scream stuck behind the wedge of fear in her throat as she forced her hands to the ground, trying to suck in gasps of air.

"Was that really necessary, Drake?" Marshall jumped in the Lieutenant's face before sinking to his knees. Tremors ripped through her as Marshall's arms cradled her body. "Reseda, you don't physically need to breathe. It's all in your head. It's not real. Snap out of it."

Reseda rocked back and forth, grabbing at her body as she screamed for help. She gripped Marshall's arms with trembling hands. "Make it stop," she cried out through clenched teeth, her cheeks puffing with each wave of pain.

"It's already stopped." Marshall raised one of her arms in front of her eyes. His voiced softened to a calming whisper. "Look, it's all gone. It was never really there."

Pain no longer pricked at her from every angle. The pitching and rolling of nausea in her stomach subsided to nothing. Anxiety that had ripped through her body, riddling her limbs with numbness, dissipated. The scrapes of skin torn by her nails healed as if her flesh had never been touched. Beautiful silence broke the scratching in her ears. Emptiness once again settled in her soul. Like always, her insides returned to the hollow shell she carried around.

She felt nothing. Remembered nothing. She was once again Reseda Juarez, super-soldier. Cold. Dead. Unfeeling. Ready to stop the war the wolves launched on humanity.

Reseda stared at her arm and tilted her head. Like waking from a dream, her mind clouded with confusion. "Marshall?"

"Right here, baby girl. It's okay." Marshall brushed a hand to her head with a soft smile.

"Why the hell am I on the ground? And I'm not your baby girl." She pushed him from her personal bubble with a hard shove. When they got back to the base, she planned a full-on intervention with him on the irrational use of misplaced romantic monikers.

Drake grunted and grabbed hold of Marshall by the upper arm. "Back to the lab. Now," he demanded before glancing down at Reseda. "*Deleo.*"

She replayed the word *deleo* in her head. Destroy. All other thoughts fell away but the need to kill. The need to vanquish the wolves.

Reseda shot to her feet as she shook her wrist, shooting a silver stake from her bracer into her palm. Her eyes glazed over as she snapped her head to look at Marshall. His face contorted, and fear filled his eyes.

Why was he afraid? She would protect him. She would protect all of them from the wolves.

"Someday she's going to remember these mind games you play on her. That kind of mental conditioning doesn't come without side effects. And I hope I'm there the day she kicks your ass," Marshall said before spitting at Drake's feet and taking off down the hill.

"What's he talking about?" Reseda turned to Drake. "What the hell was he talking about?" Marshall's words stuck in her head. If she still had feelings, she'd probably call the irritating twitch in her belly *worry*. But that was impossible now. Yet the twitch flickered its way through her like an annoying bug she couldn't quite squash.

"None of your concern. *Deleo,*" Drake demanded before following Marshall down the hill.

Reseda launched into a run, weaving among the trees. Her eyes focused on the forest floor, searching for traces of paw prints. The last of the pack must have retreated into the woods. She stopped at the base of a tall redwood.

Calloused, dirt-laden fingers clamped over her mouth from behind, while another hand dug into her waist, pinning her to a tree. "What have we here?" The man's gravelly voice vibrated in her ears. "Looks to be a pretty little snack. Just in time, too. I was beginning to waste away from hunger."

He leaned in and sniffed as he pulled her neck taut to expose his target. "You're not human. Are you a v—" Jumping back, his eyes widened as he shifted to wolf form.

Before he could finish his thought, she pounced on him, digging her fingers deep into his fur until they pressed along his spine. His pulse thudded against her palm as she squeezed until the crack of his snapped neck triggered her fingers to release. The limp body fell from her hands, bursting to dust before ever hitting the ground.

"No, I'm not. And I'm not that, either," she said and took off down the hill.

Shrieks and squeals rang out from the forest floor. She spied the Dolls in the darkness, under attack and at a disadvantage. Ambush. The only thought in her mind was to protect her girls. Once upon a time, fear for her friend's lives would have driven her to the fight. Now, obligation and training kicked in her reflexes. Like automatic muscle memory.

Reseda sped up and leapt into the air. Feet first, she thrust with all her might into the back of a wolf, knocking him to the ground. She slammed her boot against the base of a tree, and a silver spike sprung from her heel as she forced it into the spleen of the creature under her. A shrill howl hung in the air as his body disintegrated.

"Teagan," Reseda shouted, scrambling up from the ground as she ran to her partner.

Reseda extended her arms as Teagan glanced up and nodded, grabbing hold of them. Reseda braced herself as Teagan swung her up toward the approaching assailant. She lodged the exposed silver spike from her heel into his chest, causing him to explode in a cloud of dust. Reseda landed seconds later where the wolf's body once stood.

Teagan's abilities almost matched Reseda's for speed and punches. Reseda shot up from the crouched landing, tossing a "thank you" to her cohort. They took off toward the other wolves attacking Dahlia. The newest of The Dolls—while deadlier than any human could imagine—Dahlia still needed training to develop into the machine the government required.

Teagan and Reseda ran like speeding trains before leaping into midair. Each eyed their next target as they soared like bullets headfirst, coming to a halt as they collided with the beasts.

Reseda rolled to the ground, wrapping her arms around the creature's furry body. It snarled in anger as she struggled against her hold. A shrill, banshee-like shriek echoed from her throat as she strained to break free. Wetness seeped through Reseda's jeans as they rolled through the damp grass until she topped her. She withdrew a small silver dagger sheathed between her breasts and plunged it into the wolf's heart. Violent spasms ransacked her body before she grayed to dust under her, and Reseda collapsed to the ground with a thud.

She looked over to Teagan, who extinguished her victim as well. Teagan offered Reseda a hand and pulled her up from the grass. Reseda surveyed the damage around them, giving a quick nod to her second in command. They were a team—a lethal one, at that—so in tune they could just about read each other's minds.

Dahlia wiped dirt from her face and shook it from her auburn locks. "We were ambushed. There had to have been about twenty of 'em. Out of nowhere," she said in a slow southern drawl. She slid an arm across her lips, smearing blood on her face.

Teagan realigned her broken jaw with an audible pop. The bones adjusted and set back into place as if they had never been touched.

"Yours were the decoys to split us up, apparently. They were on to us. Something got leaked," Reseda replied, stepping up to brush a smudge of dirt from Teagan's light brown cheek. Her skin should have been warm, but she was just as dead inside as Reseda. For a moment, she imagined her alive, with a deep blush shading her stunning cheekbones.

She dropped her hand from Teagan's face and clenched her fists. Something got leaked all right, and Reseda grappled with the truth of who, more than likely, was the source of it. Drake would have her ass for relying on a demon's word. Reseda shook her head and ground her teeth, unable to form words from the jumbled thoughts in her head.

"We have to get back to base and let Drake know," Dahlia said, tugging at Teagan's elbow.

"You coming?" Teagan asked, sliding out from under Dahlia's hand.

Reseda forced a smile. "Yes, I'll be there in a bit."

But first, she had to go a couple rounds with a demon.

Don't stop now. Keep reading Mystic Owl books with your copy of THUNDERSTRUCK by Wren Michaels.

Don't miss the next book in the *Southwest Supernatural Society series* from E.L. Adams coming soon.

Until then, discover THUNDERSTRUCK, by City Owl Author, Wren Michaels!

Reseda Juarez is dead.

Though she functions as a human, inside she's an emotionless weapon, trapped between the living and the undead. Cold and unrelenting, she's used as a super-soldier by the government in a special task force to hunt preternatural beings to the brink of extinction.

One night, five years ago, Kane killed an innocent and his brother lost the love of his life. The aftermath forces Kane to become the alpha of the legendary Thunderbirds. He now must protect what's left of his family from the tribe of wolf shifters who ripped them apart.

When Reseda's mother is bitten by a wolf, she and Kane are forced to work together to find the Mayan Pul Yah stone to heal her—the same stone that gifted Reseda to the life she now lives. But the journey is riddled with more than the wolves, also searching for the stone.

Something strange happens to their powers when they're together, and they struggle to fight the intense attraction between them. The deeper they go, the more secrets unravel, until love is the only thing that can defeat an enemy no one saw coming.

Please sign up for the City Owl Press <u>newsletter</u> for chances to win special subscriber-only contests and giveaways as well as receiving information on upcoming releases and special excerpts.

All reviews are **welcome** and **appreciated**. Please consider leaving one on your favorite social media and book buying sites.

For books in the world of romance and speculative fiction that embody Innovation, Creativity, and Affordability, check out City Owl Press at <u>www.cityowlpress.com</u>.

ACKNOWLEDGMENTS

This story wouldn't have happened without the support of my husband! Writing is all encompassing and when I get into the zone, the kids gotta be fed I guess. And the dogs. I'm incredibly thankful that I have a partner who supports every one of my wild ideas and never lets me think I can't do it.

A HUGE thanks for Heather and Tina from City Owl Press. They are the easiest people to work with and champions for their authors. I've loved watching the stories coming out of the Mystic Owl line and NOW I HAVE ONE TOO! It feels so cool!

Theresa—If I could hug you, I would. Working through edits on this story was fun. Sometimes edits can be brutal but you made this story even better and I am so thankful. Plus, you know it's a good match when you have me LOLing over comments. I can't wait to continue this series with you!

ABOUT THE AUTHOR

E.L Adams is an avid reader of
romances and new to the paranormal romance world. A firm
believer in the HEA, she's either
enjoying life with her family or
escaping into a book. She resides
in the Southwest and loves using
the rich and vibrant landscape for
her stories.

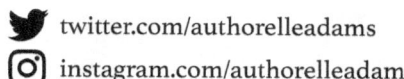 twitter.com/authorelleadams

instagram.com/authorelleadams

ABOUT THE PUBLISHER

City Owl Press is a cutting edge indie publishing company, bringing the world of romance and speculative fiction to discerning readers.

Escape Your World. Get Lost in Ours!

www.cityowlpress.com

facebook.com/YourCityOwlPress
twitter.com/cityowlpress
instagram.com/cityowlbooks
pinterest.com/cityowlpress